2733

Whispering Willows

Books by Elisabeth Hamilton Friermood

BALLAD OF CALAMITY CREEK

CANDLE IN THE SUN

GENEVA SUMMER

HEAD HIGH, ELLEN BRODY

HOOSIER HERITAGE

JO ALLEN'S PREDICAMENT

THE LUCK OF DAPHNE TOLLIVER

PROMISES IN THE ATTIC

"THAT JONES GIRL"

THE WABASH KNOWS THE SECRET

WHISPERING WILLOWS

THE WILD DONAHUES

Whispering Willows

Elisabeth Hamilton Friermood

Doubleday & Company, Inc.
Garden City, New York

For my niece
ANN HALE HAMILTON
—her vivid imagination delights me.

E.H.F.

Contents

Once I watched the friendship of two girls, two girls similar to Tess and Irene. The friendship seemed a fine thing to me even then. Now, years intervening, the friendship takes on new significance, enough to warrant a book about it.

E.H.F.

1. Tess and Irene

Tess dropped to her knees and, with an old knife, dug around the roots of the peony bush near the flat Langdon tombstone. The bush was doing well this spring, she thought, and was sure to have lots of flowers in a month or so, by Decoration day if May was warm.

The soil loosened to her liking, she sat back on her heels and looked up at the spot of clear blue April sky showing between the willow trees. It was going to be a nice day for the Snyder funeral this afternoon, she decided. Good thing too, for there was bound to be a big crowd, Otto Snyder having been such an important man in town. She hated to see people stand around a grave in a downpour of rain and that was so likely during the middle of April.

She tossed the knife in the basket of garden tools, stood up and brushed dirt from the front of her heavy denim work skirt, then, keeping very still, she gazed down the hill.

As far as she could see on either side there were tombstones; round ones, flat ones, small ones, large ones, plain ones, and fancy. There were monuments: angels with clasped hands, angels with hands outstretched, doves on the wing, flowers in festoons, statues of the Good Shepherd, and lambs of varying sizes. Every one was as familiar as the kitchen stove to Tess

Trumper, for Willow Hill Cemetery had been her home since she was four.

The grove of willow trees, up here on the Langdon lot, gave the cemetery its name. The trees could be seen from every spot in the graveyard and from the small white house at the gate where Tess lived with her uncle, Will Bagley, Willow Hill's caretaker.

On school days there wasn't time to come here, but every Saturday morning Tess climbed the hill to have a little visit with the Langdons, as she told Uncle Will.

A cardinal flashed past in a scarlet streak, settled on Jacob Tully's tall monument, and proceeded to whistle a tune for the whole silent community of granite and marble.

Tess smiled. "You sure liven up this place, you little old redbird, you," she said softly.

"Tess! Tess Trumper! Are you up there?" A voice called out from the potter's field side of the hill, down where the river wound in and out near the graves of the indigent.

"I'm here, 'Rene," Tess answered.

She watched her friend, Irene, climb the narrow road from the river, up past the mausoleum where the dead of the wealthy Converse family reposed, and past the crowded Siberling lot.

Head erect, body straight, the slender girl drew near, her white teeth showing in a smile for Tess. Tess smiled back and felt a warm glow of affection for the girl with whom she had grown up. She knew she could not have loved a sister more than she loved Irene Washington, and she was positive that no one understood Tess Trumper better except, perhaps Irene's mother, Stella.

"You're looking mighty pretty this morning, 'Rene," Tess said, tossing her long taffy-colored braid over her shoulder.

"There's not a girl in Allerton high school who can hold a candle to you."

Irene laughed. "You don't have to butter me up, Tessie. I'll get you out of whatever kind of a mess you've got your sewing in. What is it this time? Buttonholes or a French seam?" Her voice was low, and soft as velvet.

"I'm not sewing a thing right now. Don't be so suspicious. I've been studying a lot. Exams are in a few weeks and I'm kind of behind," Tess answered.

The girls sat on the broad, flat stone upon which were recorded the names of the entire Langdon family, murdered in 1842, the stone related.

"If you went to high school I bet *you* wouldn't get behind," Tess went on. "But, you know me, when I'm in study hall I try to concentrate on history or Latin and my mind wanders right out of doors, out here to Willow Hill. I think Uncle Will is wasting his money sending me in town to high school. Thank goodness I have just one more year and then I'll be free." She glanced down at the stone upon which they sat and sighed.

Irene shook her head. "You should make the most of your chances, Tessie. What are you going to do with your so-called freedom when you get it?"

"Well, one thing I won't be cooped up in schoolrooms all day." Tess paused. "But it will be a problem," she acknowledged, "what I'll do, that is. All I really know how to do is help Uncle Will. I can mow grass, cut weeds with a scythe, and I have a way with plants and flowers. At least that's what Uncle Will says. But I'm not very good at cooking and sewing as you well know. Your mother gave up on me in those departments long ago."

Irene frowned slightly. "Speaking of Mama, she's kind of worried. Seth brought home a note from Miss Jackson yesterday.

She asked Mama to come and talk to her. Mama's afraid she's going to say Seth won't graduate in May."

"But I thought Seth was a good student."

"He is as good as any in the eighth grade, I'd say. But you know Mama, always worrying about one of her brood. She and Papa have set a goal, that all ten of us will be common school graduates. Well I made it and now Seth is about to. I'm sure it's something else Miss Jackson wants to discuss. Maybe it's about one of the other kids. Nat's having multiplication troubles; that I know." Irene leaned back, looked up, and took a deep breath. "My, it seems ages since we were kids and went to Miss Jackson at Monroe Avenue school."

Tess nodded. "Sure does. Remember how surprised she was that first day in first grade when she discovered that you and I knew our A B C s and could read a little?"

Irene laughed, looked down at the gravestone, and rubbed her hand over the indentations of the letters. "It was right here that your mother taught us. She used to say how fortunate it was that the names of the Langdons included every letter in the alphabet. 'Point to W, Irene,' she would say, 'it's the beginning of your last name.' And 'Find T, Tessie, both of your names begin with that.'" Irene's face sobered. "My, she was a good woman, so kind to all of us Washingtons. I'll never forget her."

Tess turned away. Mama seemed very near, here under the willows where she had sat with the two girls so often, teaching them first their letters, and then, as they grew, other facts and fancies she wanted them to know.

Tess seldom went to Mama's grave, farther down the hill beside Papa's, save to keep the grass clipped and the shrubs tended. It was here, on the old A B C stone, as they had called it, that Mama was real and her true, laughing self again. Sometimes in the evening Tess fancied she could even hear her voice in the sighing, whooshing sound of the willow branches as they swayed with the wind. The whispering, swishing rustle of the leaves suggested Agnes Trumper's soft voice to Tess.

"Guess I've dallied about as long as I can," Tess said, looking up at the sun. "Got to get the chapel ready for Otto Snyder's funeral this afternoon. They are having a service out here as well as in town."

"Yes, I know. Papa dug his grave yesterday." Irene stood up. "I must get along too. I hung out Judge Milburn's wash early this morning. It should be dry by now in this sun and wind. I'd like to get it dampened down so Mama and I can do the ironing this afternoon. The judge has fifteen shirts besides everything else this week, so we'll be at it till dark I expect. Say, how would you like to ride into town with Papa and me tomorrow afternoon when we deliver the judge's wash? Mama wants me to take in a big batch of sweet rolls she's to bake for Mrs. Converse's party on Monday."

Tess rose. "I'd like to. Are you going to sing anything special in your church choir tomorrow morning?"

"Uh huh. A lovely new gospel song called 'Sing Out the Good News.' Mama and I are going to do it as a duet."

"Honest to John, Irene, I don't see how Stella does it, cares for her family, takes in washing, bakes for town folks, and sometimes even cooks and serves banquets in town and still has time to be a pillar in the Bethel Baptist Church. Stella Washington is a wonder!"

"I know," Irene agreed. "And Papa's no slouch either," she added. "He farms our few acres, helps your Uncle Will, works odd hours at the Madison Monument Works, and picks up and delivers Mama's washings. It keeps all of us Washingtons humping to fill our stomachs and buy school shoes for the kids."

Standing side by side, Tess, more than a head taller, looked down at Irene and grinned. "Never know we used to be the same size would you? We look like Mutt and Jeff in the funny paper. How's the weather down there, Jeff?"

Irene giggled. "Remember, Tess, when Uncle Will used to read us the funny paper every Sunday afternoon?"

"Sure do, in the winter, by our kitchen stove, and in the summer, right up here on the A B C stone. That reminds me. I haven't brought the funny papers over to your house for two Sundays. But you tell Seth I've saved them."

"I will. He makes a big thing out of reading them to the younger ones. Seth reads very well, with expression, I mean. You know, he'd make an awfully good preacher. Knows a lot about the Bible," Irene said proudly.

"Seth will be good at most anything he tries to do," Tess predicted.

Irene frowned. "The trouble is, he'll have to get a job as soon as he graduates. Ruth will be starting to school next fall. That'll make five Washingtons in school. Seth will have to help. No time for him to—well, to plan to do anything big. Papa thinks maybe he can get a job at the Gordon Hotel."

"Doing what?"

"Oh, working in the kitchen, I suppose, or some kind of janitor work. He wouldn't be trained for anything else."

"I wish—I wish—" Tess hesitated.

"Now don't worry about us, Tess. We get along fine. Mama says we are the best-fixed Negro family in Indiana. We got our own land and house, an even dozen in our family, and Tess Trumper and Will Bagley for our friends!" Irene touched Tess's big, red, roughened hand with her own smaller brown one. "But what's the best, Tessie, is that you and I are just girls who are friends."

Tess watched Irene as she rounded the sycamore tree, marking the edge of the potter's field, and disappeared at the bottom of the hill. Dear Irene, so sweet and gentle, and as beautiful as a golden-brown autumn leaf!

Never would Tess forget the first day she and Mama came here to live; Mama in bed weeping because Papa had died and Uncle Will not knowing what to do with a four-year-old. Lonely and frightened, she had wandered out into the cemetery and found shy little Irene making mud pies in the road halfway up the hill.

From that day on, Willow Hill Cemetery was a place in which the two of them explored and played, and, when Mama began the sessions at the A B C stone, a place in which they learned.

There had never been anything dead about the cemetery to Tess. Her years of tending plants, mowing grass, her growing familiarity with headstones, monuments, and family plots made her feel well acquainted with all the population of Allerton, through the relatives they had brought here.

She picked up her basket and made her way down to the chapel, stretching her long legs in lengthy strides and liking the feel of muscle pull.

She dropped her basket outside the chapel door and went in. The chill of stone walls and floor touched her face. She propped the front door open and raised all the windows before taking a broom to the floor. Clouds of dust rolled back over the pews and out the open door as she swept vigorously.

The floor swept, she looked ruefully at the dust-covered pews. Drat it, she thought, she had done it again, failed to take Stella's advice, to dampen the floor first. Cleaning was such a bother, dirt just moved from one place to another. It might be easier to dig a grave than to sweep and dust this chapel. Digging was something you could get your back into.

She searched for the dustcloth she had left in a drawer under the lectern. Finding it, she began on the organ, dusting the keyboard well. Nora Quigley, the organist at the Williams Street Presbyterian Church, would raise a rumpus if she soiled her hands on it this afternoon. Tess had had more than one experience with Miss Quigley's faultfinding when a member of that church was buried. And she would be twice as particular at the burial of such an important pillar of their congregation as banker Otto Snyder. She lifted the hymnbook and dusted the musicrack. There, that should be clean enough for the persnickety Miss Quigley!

She stepped off the platform and surveyed the front pews, gray with dust. The dustcloth in her hand seemed an ineffectual weapon with which to attack all that dirt.

Tess gave the seat of her faded-blue denim skirt a whack with her hand and grinned. There was more than one way to skin a cat! She sat down heavily at the end of the first pew, pressed the shoulders of her work jacket hard against the back and slid slowly down the length of the pew.

She hopped up at the end and examined the efficiency of her effort. Not bad, just a little dust left in the corners and the top of the back. This she flicked away with her dustcloth, then began on the next pew. By the time she was three quarters through she was thoroughly enjoying the operation. Why hadn't she thought of this years ago? Think of the time she had wasted with a dustcloth and the fun she had missed.

"Tess Trumper, what on earth are you doing?" Uncle Will had entered quietly through the door near the pulpit.

Tess stopped a slide in the middle of a pew. "Doing some very thorough dusting, Uncle Will. Reckon I should send notice of this method to Washington, D.C., and get a patent on it? A lot of time could be saved in churches and chapels all over the country if they dusted this way. Watch!" She finished the pew in one scoot and gave out with a gleeful, "Whee-ee!"

Her uncle smiled tolerantly. "Guess you'll never grow up, will you, Tessie?"

"What do you mean grow up? Five feet ten should be grown up enough even for a Trumper. I'm taller than any girl in Allerton High, and a lot of the boys too!" Tess called over her shoulder as she dusted the corners of the pew.

"You know very well what I mean; grow up into a lady and not be such a tomboy."

Tess turned and looked at the man with fond eyes. "Now see here, Uncle Will, you can't have everything. What will it be, a grass mowing, weed-cutting, tree-trimming, snow-shoveling, wood-chopping, stove-tending assistant or a lady who sews a fine seam? Name your poison!"

Uncle Will laughed. "Well, just say I want a *lady* who likes to work in Willow Hill Cemetery."

"If I can still dust pews with the seat of my skirt, I'm your lady. This discovery is too good to discard."

Uncle Will threw up both hands. "I give up." He grew sober. "Sure wish your mother was still around, though. Afraid I'm not much good at raising a young girl."

Tess walked toward him. "You are so. And don't forget I have Stella. Between the two of you I get enough advice to raise two girls."

"Yes. We couldn't have come this far without your mother if it hadn't been for Stella. She took you under her wing like one of her own. Don't know what I would have done if the Washingtons hadn't been our neighbors."

"I saw Irene this morning up at the willows. I'm going into town tomorrow afternoon with her and Sam. All right?" Her uncle nodded. "Should I get out the extra folding chairs?"

"Yes. Set them up along the side and in the back. Be a big crowd this afternoon. Newspapers have been full of Mr. Snyder's sudden death."

"His daughter, Ottilee, is in my English class. She's kind of snooty, but very beautiful and wears lovely clothes. Too bad for her, though, losing her father," Tess remarked sympathetically. "What undertaker has the funeral?"

"Adolph Riker."

"Good. It'll be a nice funeral. He always does a good job."

At half-past two that afternoon, Tess, attired neatly in a pink-checked gingham with white collar and cuffs, a jacket around her shoulders, stood outside the chapel and watched a team of bay horses draw the black shining hearse of the Riker undertaking establishment along the road and through the gate. A buggy arrived in front of the chapel well ahead of the hearse and plump Adolph Riker jumped out and smiled at her.

"Everything ready, Tess?"

"Ready, Mr. Riker. I've got the racks up in front for the flowers. I expect there are a lot."

"Biggest floral display we've ever had!" the undertaker said proudly. "But then Allerton only has one Otto Snyder. Where's Will?"

"At the grave, making a last check. He doesn't want any kind of a hitch there."

Mr. Riker nodded approvingly. He went inside the chapel, took a quick look and came out. "Tess, will you stand up there in front and tell the men how to place the flowers as they bring them in? I always count on your arrangements."

"Yes, Mr. Riker."

It was hard to believe that the tall young woman with the thick blond braid crowning the top of her head and the white

organdy collar circling her throat could be the same hoydenish
girl who had dusted these pews with the seat of her skirt a few
hours before. No one knew better than Tess Trumper that a
burial was a serious affair and that for one to run smoothly she
and Uncle Will must carefully check all details of the inter-
ment at Willow Hill.

Over the years the town's three undertakers had grown to
depend on her, especially where flowers were concerned. She
was proud of their confidence.

The flowers and casket in place, the chapel crowded to ca-
pacity, Tess stood in the back where she could see Ottilee seated
in front between her mother and grandmother. The three were
dressed completely in black, with heavy crepe veils over their
faces. A continual sobbing could be heard above Miss Quigley's
organ music. Tess couldn't tell if it came from Otto Snyder's
wife, daughter, or mother.

How many times Tess had listened to sorrow roll back
through this chapel like waves on a shore, as the bereaved
wailed out their complaints to God, questioning His right to
take their loved ones.

At the graveside Tess watched Ottilee hold onto her mother's
arm for support as the casket was lowered. Mrs. Snyder, herself, stood straight and firm and shook off the hand of Ottilee's
older brother on the other side. The elder Mrs. Snyder, her
head bowed, sat on a chair placed especially for her.

The minister picked up a little soil, dropped it in the grave
and said, "Dust thou art, to dust returneth." Then a strange
thing happened. Mrs. Snyder dislodged Ottilee's hand, threw
her veil up from her face and bent down. The minister paused,
the crowd about the grave looked on in amazement as the widow
picked up a handful of dirt, stepped to the grave's edge and let

it trickle onto the coffin. The silence was so complete that Tess could hear the plop as it fell.

Mrs. Snyder's face was pale and her eyes dry. Certainly, Tess thought, this was odd graveside behavior. Widows wept and wailed and clung to the strong arm of a close male relative. The elder Mrs. Snyder lifted her veil and eyed her daughter-in-law with red, baleful eyes.

2. Lincoln Johnson

"How was church?" Uncle Will asked as Tess came into the kitchen.

"As usual. Reverend White said to tell you he missed you." Tess put the Sunday paper she had purchased on the table and tied an apron about her waist. "Oh, good, you put the potatoes on." She took a lid from a kettle on the stove and stuck the stewing chicken with a fork. "Dinner should be ready in half an hour."

Uncle Will sat in the slat-backed rocker by the window, the thick Sunday paper on his lap. He put on his spectacles, pulled the brightly colored funny sheet from the top, and dropped it on the floor. "Well, let's see what President Taft's been doing." He rattled the paper before concentrating on the front page. "I declare, Washington news is certainly dead since T.R. left the White House. Wish now I had voted for Bryan. If he had been elected, things might have turned out livelier. Say, it says here we should be able to see Halley's comet pretty soon." He cleared his throat. "Been a lot of folks worried that the end of the world will come when it gets here."

Tess laughed. "No need to worry about that. I stopped at the library last week and looked up Mr. Halley. He was an English astronomer way back in the seventeenth century. He saw this same comet in 1682. He was so smart that he predicted it would be seen again in 1759, 1835, and 1910. The first two predictions proved right and the world's still here, so I'm sure that old comet will come along this year and not disturb a thing."

"Of course." Uncle Will went on reading.

Tess set the plates and silverware on the table. She wished she could learn Stella's knack with biscuits, but it was no use, hers turned out like rocks every time. Trying again would be a waste of flour. She sighed and took a loaf of store-bought bread from a covered crock and sliced it.

The telephone rang as she put the bread on the table. Uncle Will rose to answer. Standing at the telephone on the wall near the door, he took the pencil dangling at the end of a string and poised it over the small tablet on the telephone shelf, before he removed the receiver.

Tess listened as she hunted the potato masher, trying to make out from Uncle Will's side of the conversation who had died in town.

"Well, now, John, there's only one grave left on that lot," he said, making notes on the tablet. "Wants the baby put at the foot of the mother's grave? All right. Sam and I'll have them ready. What time's the funeral?"

He looked at Tess as he hung up the receiver. "Jake Manly lost his wife and new baby last night. That man's had more bad luck. Just three years ago the first Mrs. Manly died, two years ago he lost his father and mother, then a little girl and now this. You tell Sam when you go over there this afternoon. We'll dig the graves first thing in the morning. There's only five graves on the Manly lot so the baby's grave will have to be put at Mrs. Manly's feet. What a pity, what a pity!" Uncle Will clicked his tongue sympathetically and returned to his rocker.

"Steven Manly is in my history class," Tess remarked, vigorously attacking the potatoes with the wooden masher. "He's smart, but sort of shy. I expect that's because he's had so much trouble in his family."

After dinner Tess washed the dishes and Uncle Will finished reading the Sunday paper. The dishes dried, she took the water bucket outside to the pump and filled it. Back in the kitchen she removed her apron and rolled down her sleeves.

"Finished with the funny paper, Uncle Will?"

"Uh huh. Here it is." He retrieved it from the floor and handed it to Tess.

"I'll take it along with the other two I've saved for the Washingtons."

The funny papers under her arm, Tess walked up the hill toward the willows. She buttoned her jacket against a chill wind, and stopped halfway up at the Snyder lot where a flower-covered mound marked the banker's new grave. Would Ottilee be in school tomorrow? she wondered. What went on in the Snyders' fine big house there in town on Linden Avenue? She couldn't even imagine living in a place with so many rooms. And now there were only four of them, Ottilee, her brother, mother, and grandmother, to rattle around in the huge house like four pebbles in a lard can.

She wondered what kind of planting they would do here. She stepped over and pulled a few wilted flowers from the fancy urn at the head of the grave and threw them in the refuse box by the road. She would get up early in the morning and remove more of these, they'd be in bad shape by then. Some of the Snyders might be out tomorrow and dead flowers on a grave made such a visit even more depressing.

Her head erect, she continued the ascent, her eyes on the green willows at the top. They swayed with the wind in the afternoon sun. Some people called them weeping willows and she supposed that was appropriate here in the cemetery where there was weeping almost every day. But the name did not suit her own associations with this clump of trees.

"Listen to the rustle of them," Mama used to tell her and Irene. "Turn on your imaginations and hear the songs and stories they are whispering."

Tess sighed as she reached the top and paused. If Mama had had a chance to go to high school she might have become a poet or have written a book, she was so full of ideas about the wonder and beauty of the world. What was she, Tess, going to do with the education she was receiving? Mama, with such a chance, would have done so much better, she was sure. It was too bad Irene wasn't the one going to high school and she, Tess, the one working at washing and ironing and all the other jobs Irene did to help feed and clothe the many Washingtons.

The world was a queer place sometimes; opportunity so often knocked on the wrong doors.

She sat on the A B C stone and read today's funny paper. The adventures of the Katzenjammer Kids, Happy Hooligan, and Buster Brown were as much a part of Tess's Sunday as church and chicken for dinner.

The new funny sheet finished, she rolled it with the other two and walked down the main road on the other side of the hill to the well-worn path through the potter's field toward the Washingtons'.

In this part of the cemetery Tess tried to give special attention to the graves of the destitute. Here there were no headstones, no monuments, no plantings by sorrowing relatives. More often than not, there was not even a wooden name marker.

With all the work in the rest of the cemetery, Uncle Will had little time to spend here. It had been Agnes Trumper who had suggested years ago that Tess and Irene fix up the grave of a baby buried there by some temporary inhabitants of shantytown on the other side of the river.

That was the beginning. Now Uncle Will said he imagined Willow Hill had the best-kept potter's field in the state. The grass was cut, the wooden markers kept upright, and, in well-chosen spots, there were bushes and perennials, green and blooming, the latter started from slips taken from healthy plants on lots of the affluent. It pleased Tess that the snowball bush down here was doing as well as its parent plant on the hill. The potter's field provided excellent practice for Tess's talented green thumb.

Passing briefly by the river and on up the hill back of the Brubaker farm, Tess came in sight of the neatly painted house that had meant warmth, understanding, and love to her for many years; even more so since the death of her mother.

A big, long-eared hound came bounding out to meet her, barking a welcome.

"Good dog, Tige." Tess rubbed the animal's head fondly. The expected caress received, the dog ran back toward the house to announce her arrival. The young Washingtons, from thirteen-year-old Seth down to three-year-old John, came dashing down the path.

"Did you bring funny papers, Tessie?" Five-year-old Ruth wanted to know as she grabbed Tess's skirt and eyed the roll of papers.

"Ruthie, mind your manners." Ten-year-old Miriam reprimanded. "Tess just got here."

"Sure I brought them, Ruthie. Here, you give them to Seth. Careful now, don't unroll them." Tess looked down into the child's smiling face.

"What do you say?" Miriam pursued her sister's manners relentlessly.

"Thank you, Tessie."

"You're very welcome, honey." Tess bent down and gave the little girl a hug. "Why, Danny, isn't that a new shirt?" she asked the little boy pushing near to be noticed.

"Yep. Wore it to Sunday school and Mama let me keep it on." Four-year-old Danny touched the front of his blue calico shirt with appreciative fingers.

"I got new shoes, Tessie. See." Seven-year-old Naomi stuck out a foot. "I can keep them on this afternoon if I be careful."

"Oh, so shiny, Naomi! They're beautiful." Tess admired the high, laced shoes.

"Why don't you kids quit crowding Tess," Seth said as Joe and Nat squirmed nearer to speak to the visitor. "Here, give me the funny papers, Ruthie. We'll all sit on the steps and I'll read to you."

Tess laughed. "Oh, Seth, I like to be crowded. You Washingtons take the place of the family I don't have. How are things at Monroe Avenue school?" She asked him.

Seth's eyes met hers and a shadow clouded his alert face. "Well, I thought everything was fine. But Friday Miss Jackson had me bring a note to Mama. Wants to talk to her. I don't know what I've done or haven't done. She didn't tell me."

"Don't worry, Seth," Tess replied. "I'm sure there's nothing wrong. Hello there, Stella," she called out as the mother of this large family came to the edge of the porch with baby Rachel in her arms.

"Well, if it isn't our Tessie! Missed you, honey. Come on in and tell us what life's been doing to you. Johnny! Let loose of her skirt! You hear? That's Tessie's Sunday dress! Miriam, take that boy in hand!"

Tess left the children and looked up at the ample-figured woman with the chubby, contented baby on her hip. Tess had seen many famous paintings of mothers and their children. She wished she could paint this one of Stella and baby Rachel. Stella personified competent motherhood as far as Tess was concerned. The broad face was a warm golden-brown with large dark eyes that could look deep into a child's troubles with understanding and comfort or could flash with indignation as she punished him for a misdemeanor.

"Stella, I smell your rolls clear out here," Tess said, mounting the steps.

The big woman laughed and the baby gurgled, pleased with the jiggling movement of her mother's body. "You don't need to hint. I 'spect there's an extra one for you. Come on in. Irene's packing them to take to town."

The big table in the middle of the roomy kitchen was almost covered with flat, tin baking sheets filled with the famous Stella Washington rolls.

"Mama, they're still too warm to cover," Irene said, throwing Tess a smile of greeting.

Stella nodded. "While you're waiting, butter one from the family pans on the cabinet for Tessie." She put baby Rachel on the floor and gave her a tiny rag doll.

"I really shouldn't be eating this," Tess said as she took the small sweet roll from Irene. "I finished my dinner not over an hour ago. But it would take someone with an iron will to ever refuse one of these. Stella, if you had a bakery in town you could make a million dollars, more or less." She bit into the delicacy appreciatively.

Stella opened a cabinet drawer and took out a stack of snowy white cloths. "Maybe so, maybe so. Howsomever, nobody could take care of a bakery and my big flock too. I might make money in town, Tessie," she said, smiling, "maybe not quite a million dollars, but Mrs. Converse has offered me plenty to come to work full time for her. But the Lord's seen fit to bless Sam and me with a house, land, and good children, so I'll stay here and tend to them. Every child deserves to have his mama in the house when he comes home. I aim to be here when mine come. For a young one, knowing Mama is waiting at home, is like you and me knowing the good Lord's in heaven waiting for us. And it's a mighty comforting feeling." She handed the cloths to Irene.

"Mama, if Mrs. Converse asks me to help serve at her party tomorrow, will it be all right to say yes?" Irene asked. She tested the rolls with a finger, then covered them with the cloths.

Stella looked at Tess and winked. "I reckon so; but since she's got permanent help for Sarah May now, I doubt if she'll need you too."

"Maybe not." Irene removed her apron.

Tess wondered about the wink, but said nothing.

Stella looked approvingly at Tess's hair with the thick braid wound about her head. "Your hair looks nice this way. You're getting too old to let it hang down your back."

"I know, Stella, that's what you told me before." Tess wrinkled her nose, then laughed. "And I promise I'll put it up whenever I have time. But it *is* a bother."

"Won't hurt you a mite to get up fifteen or twenty minutes earlier before you go to school. Imagine going to high school, looking like a child!" Stella scolded.

"Stella! Whoever heard of a child as tall as I am? Anyway, nobody at high school even knows I'm there, let alone whether my hair is up or down." Tess shrugged.

"Well, *you* know you're there and I want you to walk with dignity. And don't let me hear a word of complaint about how tall you are. If I catch your shoulders slumping to make out like you're shorter, I'll box your ears, Tess Trumper. Your mama would want me to." Stella put her hands on her hips and nodded emphatically. "Two things I aim to do before I die," she went on, "make you proud to be tall and my own young ones proud to be black. The Lord breathed life into all of us. I figure He breathed a little harder on some of us, so our skins are darker. We're filled with more of His spirit too, because of it." Stella chuckled. "Law me! I sound for all the world like a preacher, don't I? How was Mr. Snyder's funeral?"

Tess told of the crowd, the flowers, the music, and of the unusual behavior of the widow at the graveside.

Stella clicked her tongue. "Probably just out of her mind with sorrow," she commiserated. "Didn't know what she was doing, more than likely. Poor thing, only two children to comfort her."

"But she has a fine house and lots of money," Tess reminded her.

"Not much comfort in those."

The kitchen door opened and Sam filled the doorway "Hello there, Tessie. You girls about ready? The wagon's hitched up."

"Oh, Sam, I'm supposed to ask you. Can you help Uncle Will in the morning? Mrs. John Manly and her new baby died last night."

Sam nodded. Stella shook her head and murmured, "Amidst joy cometh sorrow into every home alike. May the Lord give them strength to bear their burdens."

"Sam," Tess said as the wagon proceeded along Main Street, "I ride this way on the streetcar every day, but it looks different when I ride with you."

Sam laughed. "Well that old streetcar goes zooming along so fast, you can scarcely get your breath I 'spect, let alone see the houses. But this old mule of mine gives you plenty of time to see everything. Get along there, Zeke, you lazy old coot. Think we got all day?" He slapped the reins on the mule's back.

"Oh, Papa, let him take his time," Irene said. "It's such a lovely spring day with the leaves coming out. I enjoy just poking along, don't you, Tess?"

"Uh huh. Sam, remember when we were little and you would bring us to town and we always sat in the back and hung our legs out?"

Sam nodded. "And once you hopped down without me knowing, skipped over to the sidewalk, and walked along four or five blocks before I missed you." He glanced across at the girls. "Sure do wonder where them two little barefoot girls went. They surely can't be these two grown-up ladies beside me, one getting a fine education and the other almost as good an ironer and cook as her mama."

"Papa, will we have time to stop and see Grandma Barker?" Irene asked.

"We'll take time. Your mama will want to know how she's making out. We'll stop there after we've delivered the Milburn wash and the rolls and collected the three washings on the north side."

Tess watched the slowly-passing scene through half-closed eyes: frame, front-porched houses; corner groceries at intervals; brick sidewalks overhung with budding maple branches; children playing; families out for leisurely Sunday walks; buggies passing Sam's mule with a clatter of hoofs on the bricks; an occasional streetcar clanging by, making Zeke prick up his ears —this was Allerton's South Main Street, full of interest and excitement to the girl who lived at Willow Hill.

Sam pulled Zeke to a stop at the side door of the Converse home. Whenever Tess read a story that mentioned a fine house this one always came to mind. With its two front towers, each circled with long windows on three floors; its various porches with curlicued, carved railings; fine lace curtains at every window; a fountain gracing the spacious front lawn as well as an iron deer—well, it was no wonder Allerton residents spoke of it as the Converse mansion.

Sam handed Tess the reins and got down as did Irene. They carefully lifted pans of rolls from the back of the wagon.

Tess watched them as they stood on the small porch and rang the bell. The door was opened by a nice-looking young man in a white jacket. Irene and Sam disappeared inside, reappeared shortly and carried in the remaining rolls.

"Does Mrs. Converse want you tomorrow?" Tess asked when they returned. Irene nodded as Tess went on, "Did you see Sarah May? She isn't sick, is she? She usually answers the door."

Sam slapped the reins. "Sarah May's fine and mighty glad to have help in that big house. That young fellow you saw is her nephew from Indianapolis and Mrs. Converse has hired him to be her butler."

Tess turned to Irene. "Was he there last week when you and your mother helped Mrs. Converse?"

"Uh huh. His name is Lincoln Johnson." Irene looked dreamily over her shoulder at the house on the corner.

3. "Seth's the One"

In bed that night Tess could still hear Irene's soft voice as she spoke the name of Mrs. Converse's new butler. Why hadn't Irene mentioned him to her before? She loved that girl like a sister, one would think she would want to confide in Tess if she were in love. But of course, that couldn't be true, she had only met Lincoln Johnson once before. Still there was that wink of Stella's. Did that mean that Stella thought—? Tess punched her pillow and tossed her braid aside.

She and Irene had been together every day through the eight grades of Monroe Avenue school. And, during the three years she had been in high school and Irene had worked, they had been together at least three times a week. She knew she could never have lived through those awful days right after Mama died if it hadn't been for Irene. Just the touch of her hand brought comfort to Tess.

Now, this hint of a new interest, an interest which well might separate them, troubled Tess and kept her awake.

Doggone it! she thought, *she* hadn't paid any attention to the boys at high school, why did Irene, all of a sudden, have to discover Lincoln Johnson? Now, tut tut, there, Tess Trumper, she told herself, you know very well why you have pretended the boys weren't there; because they look right through you, can't see you at all, you are such a big, overgrown string bean!

Oh, what she wouldn't give to be little and dainty like Irene. Even Ottilee Snyder with her red hair and blue eyes wasn't as pretty as Irene. But then, Tess admitted to herself, she *was* prejudiced because she knew Irene's inner self too, or, that is, she had until now. Who knew what that 'Rene Washington was thinking these days? Well, she would ask her in the morning, get her to talk about that Johnson fellow! No use beating around the bush.

When her alarm clock went off at six, Tess wished she had the time she had wasted in worry the night before, had it to snuggle down and snooze in the luxurious warmth of the covers. But if she was to get breakfast, pack her lunch, inspect Otto Snyder's grave, and make the 7:30 streetcar, she'd have to hop out.

Uncle Will had the fire going briskly in the cookstove when she got to the kitchen, and the teakettle spout was sending up a white curl of steam. With her usual banging of pans and clatter of dishes Tess got breakfast, made her sandwiches, and washed the dishes; then hurried up the hill at seven to remove the dead flowers from the new grave.

At seven-fifteen she dashed out the gate, her skirts held high, and ran like a colt down the dirt road toward Four Corners, the end of the Willow Hill streetcar line. It was times like this that long legs came in handy, she thought as she approached the Madison Monument Works where the streetcar circled to go back to town.

Irene was already there, grinning, as she watched Tess race to arrive before the trolley car coming down the street.

"Whee!—I made it," Tess cried, stopping beside Irene.

"What happened to the new hairdo?" Irene asked, glancing at the long braid hanging down from under Tess's hat.

"Didn't have time, had to clean up Otto Snyder's grave just in case any of the family comes out today."

"Well, that's a good reason, so I won't tell Mama on you. Look, Tess, I'm wearing the new uniform Mama made me." Irene opened her coat and revealed a crisply starched white dress. "Mama said I should wear something else and carry it in a package, but I didn't want to wrinkle it. I've got a big apron in here to wear over it in the kitchen until it's time to serve." She held out a newspaper package.

"Hmmm. You look good enough to eat." Tess looked at her speculatively. "Now, little 'Renie, tell me about Sarah May's nephew. You have been holding out on Aunt Tessie, young lady!"

Irene buttoned her coat self-consciously and put the package under her arm. At that moment the streetcar pulled around the circle and stopped. The girls climbed aboard at the back.

"Good morning, Mr. Cooper," Tess greeted the uniformed conductor on the platform.

"Morning, Tessie. Hello, Irene. How are all the Washingtons?"

"Fine, thank you."

The girls sat at the front end of the car. Three other passengers got on. The conductor reached up, pulled the bell cord twice as a signal to the motorman up front, and the trolley car lurched forward along Main Street.

"Now," said Tess, settling her lunch and history book on her lap, "what about Lincoln Johnson?"

"Well, you saw him. What do you want to know?"

Tess frowned impatiently. "Oh, Irene, don't be so hedgy. I saw the look in your eyes yesterday. Has he talked to you? Does he like you? What kind of a person is he? I'm not sure I like you working there without Stella."

Irene smiled and leaned nearer to be heard above the rattle of the car. "Don't be a fuss budget. You know how careful Mama is about places I work. Mama thinks he's real nice. He talked more to her when we were there than he did to me. Sarah May calls him Linc."

"What do you call him?"

"I haven't talked to him enough to call him anything—yet. Mama says he's very smart, graduated from high school in Indianapolis, and worked down there as assistant chef in one of the big hotels. He visited Sarah May in February and Mrs. Converse persuaded him to work for her. When Sarah May has one of her bad spells of rheumatism he takes over the cooking. She says he's very good at it. He knows how to drive an automobile too, drives Mrs. Converse all over town in hers."

Tess tightened her mouth and shook her head. "It sounds to me as if this Lincoln Johnson is just too good to be true. Don't you be gullible and get taken in by his city education. Remember you are just a country girl and not on to the ways of the world."

Irene burst out laughing. "Tessie Trumper, you are a riot! What stories have you been reading lately? And what gives you the idea that you are an expert on the intentions of young men?"

Tess grinned. "Well, you watch your step anyway." She looked out the window. "Next street's mine. I'll be over tonight to hear all about your day. And I'll want to know what Miss Jackson has to tell Stella, too," she added.

Tess stood on the curb and watched the streetcar pull away. She crossed the street and continued on Danbury toward Allerton high school three blocks beyond. She glanced up at the clock on the school tower. Five minutes to eight, she might have time to finish copying the English paper on Milton before the eight-thirty bell if she hurried. She extended her stride, passing other students along the way.

"What's all the rush, Tess?" a girl called as Tess passed her. Tess slowed down. "Oh, hi there, Donna. Got a paper to finish copying."

"Come on, walk with me. It's early."

Tess adjusted to the slower pace. "Finish your history reading?"

"No. But I did finish *Les Misérables* for my book report. Going to give it orally for Miss Eben after school this afternoon. Pray for me. I liked the book but I just know she'll ask something I won't remember." Donna stopped. Tess looked at her questioningly. "Say, look! Coming there on Ripley Street! It's Ottilee! Hmmm, isn't that new black coat of hers lovely? Say, I bet there was a crowd out at your cemetery when her father was buried Saturday." Tess nodded.

Donna continued. "My mother heard from a friend who lives on their street, that Saturday night Ottilee's mother took a room at the Gordon Hotel! Mama says she doesn't believe it. But it might be so. We heard that she and Ottilee's grandmother never did get along." They watched the girl in black cross the street and continue in front of them.

"I didn't think she would be back to school today," Tess remarked. "But then I expect she's glad to come back if there's quarreling at home. I wonder what they're fighting about. You'd think with all they have, things would run smoothly."

"You can never tell about rich people," Donna answered. "Maybe they are fighting over all that money Mr. Snyder left."

In her home room, Tess dipped her pen in the inkwell, copied the last few lines of her theme on Milton, folded the sheets lengthwise, and wrote on the outside,

Teresa Trumper
English VI
April 18, 1910

During the third period, in English class, Tess eyed Ottilee on the other side of the room. The black dress accented the pallor of her skin and the titian brilliance of her hair. Her eyes were lowered and her hands twiddled a pencil absent-mindedly. Tess thought it was nice of Miss Eben not to call on Ottilee to recite.

Looking about at the other students, Tess could identify each one with a lot at the cemetery where members of his family lay. Every boy and girl in this class was a part of her Willow Hill, she thought. Each carried on certain characteristics, ideas, and attitudes of those who had gone before, mingling them with the different ones he acquired on his own, so that he appeared to be a new individual. But, Tess wondered, was he?

Was there really anything new in the world? Wasn't all new knowledge just a rearrangement and a more complete understanding of things that had been around all the time? For all of her own advantages in these modern times, she didn't feel a bit smarter than the quiet ones resting at Willow Hill. If only she could somehow carry on Mama's creative and poetic nature. She couldn't remember Papa, but from what she had been told, she felt she was more like him than Mama. Jimpson Trumper, a giant of a man, had been a forthright, honest blacksmith, using his muscles to advantage; but Papa, Tess knew, was not much in the thinking department.

"Teresa." Miss Eben was looking at her. Tess blinked her eyes. Oh, dear, she hadn't been listening. What was she going to ask? "Teresa, tell something of Milton's part in the Civil War in England."

Tess swallowed and tried to remember what she had written in her paper. Miss Eben always seemed to catch her when her mind was woolgathering. But she *had* studied, she was sure she knew this if she could just sort out her thinking, separate her reading from Willow Hill thoughts.

"Well, Teresa!"

"When King Charles I was beheaded, Oliver Cromwell set up the Commonwealth." She paused, watching the teacher's face for a sign of approbation.

"Yes, yes. Go on."

Tess closed her eyes momentarily, trying to recall the words on that page. "Milton had worked hard for Cromwell's Puritan party, so Cromwell rewarded him with the job of Latin Secretary to the Council of State." Tess blurted the words out quickly, fearful that they might elude her unpredictable brain.

"That's right. Latin at that time, was the written language of diplomacy in Europe," Miss Eben said. "Now, Ralph, tell me something of Milton's home life."

Tess heaved an inaudible sigh of relief. Her moment of torture was over, now she could return to her own thoughts. She was glad *she* didn't have to tell of Milton's home life. For all of his education, religion, and poetic genius, he had been a terrible husband and father. Milton had unhappy wives and bitter, selfish children, the book said. Too bad he hadn't had a Sam Washington around to give him a few pointers on a happy family, Tess contemplated, her thoughts flying from seventeenth-century England to twentieth-century Indiana in a flash.

That afternoon Tess paused at their mailbox perched on a post near the road, just outside the main gate. They seldom got any mail, but the Allerton *Morning News* was usually there.

In the house, she dropped a book and the newspaper on the table and went upstairs to change her dress and shoes. Uncle Will was not around; she presumed he and Sam were working on the Manly lot, since the burial was to have been at three o'clock.

Dressed in her working clothes, she found the men packing down the dirt on the two new mounds. Many floral pieces leaned against the Manly monument in the center.

"Ready for me to put these on?" Tess asked.

Uncle Will looked up. "Just in time, Tessie, to do your part. Sam and I are all through here."

"Did they have a service out here in the chapel?" Tess asked.

"No. They had the funeral at the Manly home and then just had a brief graveside service." Uncle Will picked up his shovel.

"That's good. Sometimes I think it's wrong to put a family through *any* kind of a service," Tess said, looking at a large wreath of pink carnations with a wide band of white satin ribbon across it upon which was written in large gold letters: FOR MOTHER AND BABY. "And all those mournful hymns they sing are just heartbreaking. Don't you think so, Sam?"

Sam raked the grass near the new graves. "Well, it all depends on how you look at it. Sometimes the words are mighty comforting. Yes sir, those good old hymns promise we'll all meet again in the sweet by and by. And sometimes that can bring a lot of peace to sorrowing folks, Tessie."

Tess began covering the mounds, one large, one small, with the floral pieces. "Well, I'd like some of those rousing gospel songs sung at *my* funeral, songs like those Stella and Irene sing in your church, Sam. I'd rather folks would tap their feet at my funeral than wipe their eyes."

Uncle Will laughed. "You see, Sam, what I got on my hands! —a rebel, a real rebel!"

Sam put the tools on the wheelbarrow and smiled at Tess fondly. "Tessie's all right, Will, just a mite touched in the head, maybe, but she'll outgrow it one of these days. Oh, yes, Tessie, Seth asked me to remind you that tomorrow's his current-event day and should he come after the paper?"

"You tell him I'm coming over right after supper as soon as Uncle Will finishes with the *Morning News.* Want to hear about Mrs. Converse's big doings. And wasn't Stella going to school this afternoon to see Miss Jackson?"

Sam nodded as he bent and took the wheelbarrow handles in his big capable hands. "She's some worried, I guess, but not me. All my children know they got to study hard. Seth's the smartest of the lot. Miss Jackson's got no cause for complaint 'bout him. Old Sam knows that for a fact."

It was dusk by the time Tess started up Willow Hill and on toward the Washingtons'. There was a brisk, cold, moist wind. She hoped there wasn't going to be one of those unexpected April snowstorms. They could be devastating to plants, so delicate this time of year. She looked at the cloudy sky. No one could see Mr. Halley's comet, even if it were up there.

Darkness covered Sam's partially plowed fields, but lamplight shone from the kitchen windows. The sound of music rolled out to Tess even before she got to the gate. She grinned to herself. Everything must be all right, for the voices of all the Washingtons were singing out rhythmically. She could hear Stella's rich contralto and Sam's deep bass leading the others.

She patted Tige and hushed him with a word as he let out one bark. He followed her to the back door, where she stood still to listen.

*"See them children dressed in white.
It must be the children of the Israelite,"*

sang Stella and Sam. The voices of the young Washingtons answered with the chorus:

*"The old ark's a-moverin', a-moverin', a-moverin',
The old ark's a-moverin' an' I thank God."*

Softly humming the loved old tune with the family, Tess remained outside until all the verses and answering choruses had been sung.

She opened the door. The lamp was in the center of the big table. Joe and Miriam were washing and drying the dishes, Seth and Nat sat at the table with books in front of them, Stella rocked beside the table, her lap full of mending; Sam, on the other side, repaired a child's shoe, the little children on the floor near his feet.

Cries of "Tessie!" came from all sides. Tige began to bark, having restrained himself as long as possible. Welcoming noises filled the kitchen.

"All right! That's enough!" Stella's firm voice brought quiet. "You want to burst Tessie's ears?"

"You folks are in fine voice this evening," Tess said, looking about. "Where's Irene?"

"Not home yet," Sam replied, holding the shoe, sole up, between his knees.

Tess glanced at the clock on the shelf above the stove. "It's after seven. Isn't it kind of late for her? I thought that was a luncheon affair. Shouldn't she be home?"

"She'll be along directly," Stella said.

Tess relaxed at the reassuring tone. She looked at Seth, pulled up a chair, and sat beside him. "Well, it's easy to see that

Miss Jackson must not have had any bad news about Seth for you this afternoon, Stella. What did she say?"

Stella and Sam looked at Seth with affectionate eyes. "Tell her, Seth," Sam said.

Seth glanced at Tess, then down at his open book. "Oh, you tell her, Mama." He stirred self-consciously on his chair.

"Well, Tessie," Stella said, pulling a china darning egg from a stocking. "Miss Jackson thinks our Seth is uncommonly smart and that he shouldn't quit school but should go on to high school next fall. Now what do you think of that?"

Tess gave Seth a hearty whack on the back. "That's the boy, Seth, old fellow! Hurray for the Washingtons!"

Seth grinned, then sobered and looked at his father. "But we're not sure I can go yet."

Sam pounded a tack in the shoe sole. "No, but we're going to give it some thought, Son, some real deep thought. It's well-nigh sixty years ago since my grandma slipped into Indiana with her little boy, my pa, both of 'em runaway slaves then. But I 'spect it's time for us to go some farther. I reckon maybe Seth's the one to raise us up a little taller. Yes sir, Tessie, we're going to think on it real hard."

"Let's sing some more," Miriam said as she closed the door after emptying the dish water.

When Irene arrived five minutes later, Tess and the Washingtons were shaking the walls with:

> "*Roll, Jordan, roll*
> *Roll, Jordan, roll,*
> *I want to go to Heaven when I die*
> *To hear old Jordan roll.*"

Irene joined in as she removed her coat and hung it in the hall closet. The last verse and chorus over, Joe began telling her what Miss Jackson had said about Seth; Miriam chimed in loudly, talking at the same time.

Irene put her hands over her ears. "Mama, what's it all about?"

Stella quieted the two and explained.

Irene stood behind Seth and tousled his crinkly hair. "Good for you, Buddy," she said, reverting to his nickname that, at ten, he had insisted they eliminate. "I'm proud of you."

Seth shook off her hand. "Oh, cut it out, 'Rene." He turned to Tess. "You brought the paper?"

"Uh huh," Tess answered. "Here you are. Front page is full of good items to choose from for your current event. Arizona and New Mexico Territories are still trying for statehood and there's another prediction about the trouble Halley's comet is going to bring."

"I talked about that comet last week," Seth said, spreading the newspaper on the table. "If it doesn't show up soon, I guess some folks are going to just be scared to death, waiting; they're so afraid it will bring the end of the world."

Stella laughed. "Well, it's filling up the churches, I'll say that. Lots of sinners and backsliders get religion when they think old man death's breathing on their necks." She looked at Irene. "Well, how did things go today, honey?"

"Just fine, Mama. Mrs. Converse would like to have me two days a week until the spring-cleaning is done. And say, your rolls melted like butter on hot pancakes. How those ladies ate them!"

Tess watched Irene wash her hands at the washpan on a stand just inside the pantry. Her white uniform was slightly wrinkled now, but her black wavy hair, parted in the middle and drawn over the tops of her ears into a small roll in the back, was still as tidy as this morning. Tess wondered why

Irene never got mussed up at work, while she, Tess, looked such a mess in so short a time.

"Mama," Irene called out as she dried her hands on the roller towel, "I invited Linc—Lincoln Johnson to come to prayer meeting on Thursday. Do you think that was all right?"

Tess watched Stella as she held up a darning needle to thread it.

"Uh huh." Stella knotted her thread. "You and him serve the lunch?"

"Yes. He knows a lot about the right way to serve. He told me several things I hadn't known before."

Stella nodded. "Yes. He's real smart, that one."

Tess had a tight feeling in her throat. Irene was thinking about that young man too much. And now, if he started going to Bethel Church and Irene went to the Converse house twice a week—!

4. "Character Development"

Walking home through the cemetery, Tess suddenly had a sense of panic. What would she do if Irene got married and left home? At high school, she had not tried very hard to make friends because she knew that Irene was always waiting for her at Willow Hill.

Irene was the only one, besides Uncle Will, to whom she had ever expressed her ambition, an ambition so unlikely ever to come true, that, being a realistic, practical person, she let herself dream of it only on rare occasions.

"If only I had a greenhouse, Irene," she would say to her friend, "a greenhouse right there across the road from Willow Hill Cemetery. I know I could make a go of it. There's money in flowers. Just look at all that's spent for them at every funeral. And the only one in Allerton is way the other side of town. Located out here, I could give the Herlemans some competition."

Now, if Irene left, and she couldn't talk "greenhouse" with her—

The gravel in the road crunched under the soles of her high, laced shoes as she descended the hill toward home. A cold mist blew on her face with sharp, needlelike jabs, but Tess didn't notice.

Next afternoon after school, Tess joined the group of students on the corner, waiting for the Willow Hill streetcar. Her pocketbook on one arm, a copy of *Silas Marner* held under the other, she gazed across the street unseeingly, her thoughts faraway.

She'd have to stop at the grocery on her way home; the bread crock was empty, and didn't they need sugar too? If she could just remember to write down when things were about gone, but it was only when Uncle Will asked for an item that she discovered they were out. What a no-good housekeeper she was! Oh, well, she couldn't attend to everything.

And now here was this book she had to read for English. She had started it in study hall and the first six pages were awfully dull, but maybe it would get better. Some books you just had to wade through for three or four chapters before you got the gist of what the author was talking about. She would never have chosen this book of her own free will, that was sure. She liked to read, but something with get-up-and-go to it, not a story about a miserly old weaver. Miss Eben had said every one in class must read it by May 2, so she would just have to dig in and plow through it.

It was probably one of those stories of character development Miss Eben was always talking about, one wherein the main person got better and better, until at the end he was just too good to be true. She wondered if there were any books about a person whose character developed the other way and he got worse and worse.

There were people like that in real life, or at least there had been, for there were a lot of them lying in Willow Hill. How many times Uncle Will had looked at an especially complimentary epitaph on a new tombstone and said, "Humph, that's about as appropriate for him as a halo for Old Nick. This fellow was an old devil from the word go!"

Tess sighed, thinking that she knew more about those lying in Willow Hill than she did about the students standing near her. Maybe she should have tried to make friends at high school. Had she been too independent? Would it have made any difference if she weren't so tall? How many people did she really know besides Irene and her family?

Well, there were the three undertakers, Adolph Riker, John Bixby, and Eli Wallace, but she knew them only in a business way, they weren't really friends. She knew Peter Madison, owner of the Madison Monument Works, had known him well since she was a child, when she and Irene had gone there to watch him work on marble and granite.

The kind of life she led was different from any girl in town. Was it right to be so different? And if she never got to know any young men, how was she ever going to get married? Until this Lincoln Johnson threat she hadn't given it too much thought. But when Uncle Will died, and die he must she knew well, what would she do?

The clang of the streetcar brought her to, and she climbed on board with the others. Seated, she saw that Ottilee Snyder sat opposite. She caught Tess's eye and gave a faint smile of recognition which Tess returned.

Tess studied the girl in black. A long, fitted coat reached almost to the bottom of Ottilee's skirt, a skirt just short enough to show a few buttons on the insteps of her shiny high shoes. Her black hat was wide-brimmed with a small ostrich feather and some velvet ribbon along the side. That must be what the ad in the paper for Miss Dailey's millinery shop called the Gainsborough hat, the latest thing from Paris, Tess remembered.

Tess wondered how she would look in a hat like that, or would she look better in one that turned up on the side. What had the ad called that style? Oh yes, the cavalier shape. She pulled her old gray felt hat of four years' vintage, down on one side and glanced at the toes of her shoes showing below her brown alpaca skirt. The soles bore witness to the muddy condition of the road from Willow Hill to the streetcar line. She pulled her feet out of sight and gave her attention again to Ottilee.

Ottilee wore black kid gloves. Tess looked closer. That book in her hand—it *was* a copy of *Silas Marner*. Tess chuckled inwardly. Education was a great social leveler. Even the beautifully dressed Ottilee couldn't escape Miss Eben's obsession with character development.

The other students got off at various streets in south Allerton. Tess wondered where Ottilee was going. When the car stopped at Jefferson Street, Ottilee crossed over and sat beside Tess.

"You live out this way, don't you?" she asked. Tess nodded. "The Monument Works is at the end of the line, isn't it?"

"Yes. Is that where you're going?"

"I'm to meet my brother and grandmother there to select a proper stone for Papa." The streetcar rumbled and shook, and the motorman stomped on the foot bell which clanged loudly.

"Your mother and grandmother, did you say?" Tess asked. This would disprove that tale Donna had told her.

"No. My *brother* and grandmother," Ottilee repeated, glancing out the window self-consciously.

So, Tess thought, Donna was right, there was something amiss in that family.

The car pulled around the circle and the two girls got off.

"Right there's the place," Tess said with a nod toward the building.

"Thank you. I see our carriage there in front."

The door to the establishment opened and a tall young man stepped out. Tess recognized Ottilee's brother. She wondered how tall he was, six feet maybe? His hair was even redder than Ottilee's.

"Hurry up, Ottilee," he called. "Don't keep Grandma waiting."

Ottilee ran down the sidewalk, calling a good-by over her shoulder.

Tess crossed the street to the grocery store. What would they put on Otto Snyder's tombstone? she wondered.

That night it happened! Tess wakened from a deep sleep. Uncle Will stood in the doorway, a lamp in his hand.

"Get up Tessie. It's here at last!"

Tess sat up and blinked her eyes. "What is?"

"Why Halley's comet, of course! Don't it beat all how a fellow way back there in the ancient times could call the shots on a heavenly body this way!"

Tess hopped out of bed and ran to the window. "I don't see it."

"Oh, you have to go outside on the other side of the house. Get some clothes on and we'll take a look."

Tess slipped into her shoes, pulled on her heavy coat, tied a fascinator on her head, and joined Uncle Will in the yard.

"Well, there she be, sailing through our sky once more right on Mr. Halley's schedule. When did you tell me it was here last?"

"Back in 1835." Tess stuck her hands in her pockets for warmth, her head upturned to the night sky, so brilliantly lighted by the comet and its shining tail. "You know, Uncle Will, that tail is millions of miles long!"

"You don't mean it!"

"Let's go up the hill a ways," Tess suggested.

They walked all the way up and stood at the edge of the willow grove. Tess looked down at the glow cast on the familiar shapes of marble and granite. Never had Willow Hill looked so beautiful, she thought. The Emersons' angel sparkled so, that Tess imagined she could see a halo around the head.

"Well, Uncle Will, we know it's not going to be the end of the world. But it *would* be a fine night for Gabriel to blow his horn and the dead to rise. They would sure enjoy coming back on a night like this." Tess lifted her eyes to the sky again.

"Fine night or no, we better get back to bed. I've got two burials coming up tomorrow. Come on."

Slowly Tess followed her uncle, glancing again and again at the awe-inspiring sight above. This was an extraordinary, bright light that had come to shine on 1910, she thought. Wouldn't it be a good idea to get a new light shining upon herself? Here she was, almost a senior, and inside she was scarcely grown up at all. Do you know what you need, Tess Trumper? she laughed to herself. You need some character development!

The comet was the chief topic of conversation for the rest of the week. Irene came over on Saturday afternoon and described how Stella and Sam had gotten all the children out of bed to look at the sky. Danny, she said, had been so disappointed he had cried.

"It's nothing but a star," he had wailed. "I thought it was a horse. Tessie said it would have a long tail."

"Oh, dear!" Tess laughed as Irene related it. "Me and my yen to show off a little learning."

"Speaking of learning," Irene put in, "what high school textbooks do you have? I think I should do some special reading. No use to stop learning just because I don't go to school."

Tess raised her eyebrows. Irene's reading usually consisted of novels Tess brought from the public library. "Linc Johnson's idea?"

Irene ignored the question, left the kitchen, and went to the living-room bookcase. "How about this *American Literature?* Think it's too much for me?" she called out.

Tess appeared in the doorway. "No. It tells about American writers and their work. I studied that last year. This year it's English Literature. But yesterday we spent the whole period talking about an American author, Mark Twain. He died on Thursday, you know." She watched Irene turn the pages of the textbook.

"Yes, Linc told me. But did *you* know, Tess, that Mark Twain said that he came in with Halley's comet in 1835 and would go out with it in 1910? And he did, just two days after it appeared."

Tess raised her eyebrows again. "Suppose Linc told you that too."

"Yes. Oh, Tess, he's so smart. Makes me wish I could have gone to high school, for one year at least." Irene turned her big dark eyes up at Tess with such emotion that Tess realized there was no doubt how her friend felt about Lincoln Johnson.

A disconcerting thought came to mind; what if he didn't care for Irene! Tess couldn't bear for her to be hurt. Perhaps she should call some day at the Converses' side door and ask him point blank what his intentions were. Well, maybe she wouldn't do that, but she *was* going to have a talk with Stella when Irene wasn't around.

"How old is this Lincoln?" she asked.

"About twenty-three."

"Kind of old for you, isn't he? You're only sixteen."

"Oh, Tessie, you know very well I'll be seventeen in June. He's not too much older. He's so different from any young man I've ever met. He's thinking about more important things than partying and baseball and just having a good time like the other fellows."

"What kind of important things?"

"He's saving his money to go into business. Living in as he does, he says he can save almost every cent he makes. He thinks it's up to every person of color to advance the position of the Negro in this country by showing what he can do in business as well as in other fields like writing and music and—and other things like that." Irene hesitated. "He called them the arts." She smiled up at Tess shyly as she put the book on the table. "You can see, Tess, how smart he is. And," she added softly, "he has the nicest smile and such broad shoulders."

"Oh, has he now?" Tess grinned tolerantly. "Did you tell him about Seth?"

"Yes indeed. He's awfully pleased. He thinks education is the answer to everything. He says all Negro children should go to high school."

"All white ones don't," Tess said, picking up yesterday's newspaper from a chair. "Remember, from our eighth-grade class of nineteen at Monroe Avenue school only eight went on to high school."

"I know. Wish I had been one of them," Irene said wistfully. "It didn't bother me before. But Linc says I can learn by myself. He says anybody who can read can educate himself if he's got enough ambition to stick at it."

Tess remembered this conversation that evening as she sat by the lamp in the living room and opened *Silas Marner*. She felt a little ashamed, complaining about dull old Silas. There was Irene, longing for the chance for an education, and here she was grumbling because of a little hard reading. Her bookmark was at the beginning of Chapter Three. She'd have to dig in if she got this read by May 2, a week from next Monday.

Next day, Sunday, was the first really warm sunny day of the 1910 spring. Afternoon brought many Allertonians to Willow Hill Cemetery; some drove out in buggies, but most came on the streetcar. Decoration Day was a little more than a month away and everyone wanted to get his lot fixed nicely before that holiday. As caretaker, Uncle Will was obliged only to keep the grass cut, the trees trimmed, and the roads in good condition. However, Willow Hill lots got many extras from Tess Trumper's apt hands.

Today she stood on their porch and watched bent and kneeling figures all the way up the hill, digging around plants and setting out new ones. If she only had that greenhouse across the road what a business she could do this time of year, she thought. These people would have to go all the way across town to the north side to buy their plants.

A man turned in at their gate. Tess recognized Judge Milburn as he limped up the path on his cane.

"Good afternoon, Judge." She descended the three steps. "How are you?"

"Hello, Tess. Oh, I'm pretty good."

"Won't you come in?" she offered.

"Too nice a day to be inside. But I'll sit here on the steps for a minute. I came to see *you*." He eased himself down on the top step, leaning his cane against his knee. "You know my lot, yon side?"

Tess nodded as she sat beside him, picturing the place where the judge's wife and three of his children lay.

"As you know, Tess, I've always enjoyed taking care of my lot. But there comes a time when one must bow to the inevitable ravages of age, my chief one being rheumatism in this dratted knee. I've watched you grow up here all these years, and I've noticed your increasing interest and skill with plants. The thought occurred to me that you might be willing to take care of my lot. I'd pay you, of course."

"I'll be glad to tend your lot, Judge," Tess replied, "but you don't have to pay me. I often work on neglected graves just because I dislike having Willow Hill appear uncared for. But nobody pays me."

"Honest work deserves honest pay. Do you think two dollars a month the year round would be enough?"

"Oh, that's too much. There would be nothing to do in the winter when snow covers everything," she protested.

The judge shook his head. "No. Two dollars a month it is, snow or no snow." He took a wallet from his pocket and removed some bills. "Here is twelve dollars in advance for the next six months. That pays you until October twenty-four." He handed over the money.

Tess took it hesitantly. "Oh, Judge, you shouldn't pay me until I've done some work. Not all this in advance!"

"The matter is closed," the judge said, the finality in his voice as decisive as the rap of his gavel in court. "It will give me a comforting feeling there in town to know that you stop by occasionally to see how Martha and the children are making out."

Tess folded the money. "I'll do my best," she said. "I've

always thought that little stone you put up for Baby Claude the dearest one in the whole cemetery."

"He was our first child. Martha designed that little stone." The judge sighed and got to his feet. "Well, Tessie, I leave them in your hands."

Tess walked with him to the gate. "Nice thing happened to the Washingtons," she told him. "Seth's teacher thinks he's so smart he should go to high school."

"Well now, that's fine. An unusual family, the Washingtons. Old Ben Brubaker couldn't have done a better thing than to will that parcel of land to Sam's grandmother. The Brubakers took her and her little boy in, you know, even though it was against the law in Indiana then to keep runaways in the state. But she repaid them, that's for certain; nursed the whole family through the smallpox when nobody else would go near the place. How they loved that woman. Old Grandma Brubaker used to say Rella Washington had been heaven sent."

Tess nodded. "Yes, Sam often tells Irene and me about his grandmother. Oh, there comes Irene now."

"Good afternoon, Judge," Irene greeted the elderly man.

"Hello, Irene. I was about to drive over to your place and pick up my washing and save your father a trip in." The judge opened the gate for Irene.

"I just told the judge about Seth going to high school in the fall," Tess remarked.

Irene frowned. "Well, I'm not at all sure about that. A sort of bad thing happened yesterday. You know that Seth takes the wagon into town every Saturday to collect the garbage from the restaurants and the Gordon Hotel for our pigs." Tess nodded and the judge paused to listen. "Well, Mr. Whitcomb, manager of the hotel, told Seth that he had a full-time job for him as soon as school is out."

"Oh, but he mustn't take it," Tess interrupted. "He isn't going to, is he?"

"Well, it's hard for a thirteen-year-old boy to refuse this kind of job, that of a bellboy; a red uniform with brass buttons goes with it." Irene shook her head. "The pay and tips Mr. Whitcomb promised seemed like all the money in the world to Seth. And it *is* a lot of money in our family. But it just doesn't seem right when Miss Jackson says Seth has an extraordinarily good mind."

The judge stirred the gravel in the road with his cane. "Is Seth at home now?" he asked.

"Yes."

"I'll have a little talk with him when I get over there." The judge turned to Tess. "Thanks, Tess, for helping me out. I probably won't be out again until Decoration Day. Any flowers you want for the lot, you just have them charged to my account. I'll tell the Herlemans that you have my permission. Good-by."

The girls watched the old gentleman limp down the road to his horse and buggy.

"What a fine man he is," Tess murmured. "He must be lonely, living in that big house with only a housekeeper, all his children married and away."

Irene nodded. "I hope Seth will listen to him. If he doesn't, I think I'll ask Linc to come out and tell that boy a thing or two!"

Tess looked sharply at Irene. Linc again! It seemed that all roads of thought led directly to that young man as far as Irene was concerned. Tess wished he had stayed in Indianapolis.

5. Irene's Beau

It rained every day during the last week in April and by the first of May, Willow Hill was green and blooming. Tess caught the streetcar each day with great reluctance, longing to stay and help Uncle Will make the cemetery beautiful for Decoration Day.

At school she tried to be more friendly. She had had a talk with Stella about Linc Johnson and Irene's interest in him. Stella had told her not to worry, Linc was a fine person, a credit to their race. Then Stella had said, "But it's *you* I worry about, honey. You should make friends with other girls. Here you've been at high school nigh unto three years and not once have you brought a girl friend home with you to spend the night or gone to anyone's house in town. It's not natural. We Washingtons love you, child, but you should have other friends too."

Tess told Donna Grant about her encounter with Ottilee Snyder. Donna reported that the informant who lived near the Snyders, had told her mother, that several trunks had been hauled away; taken, she supposed, to the hotel where Ottilee's mother was still staying. "Waiting for Mr. Snyder's will to be probated, I presume," Donna had added. "I wonder if she'll leave town then. Ottilee must feel awful with her mother and grandmother not speaking. Her brother has gone back to his college, so Ottilee has to bear the brunt of the family quarrel."

In English class Tess watched Ottilee and speculated how it would feel to be beautiful, rich, well dressed, and sought after by the boys. She wondered if she could do her hair like Ottilee's, all fluffy around her face and coiled in the back. Probably not, her own hair was as straight as a reed.

In the background of her thoughts she listened half-heartedly to the class discussion of the character development of *Silas Marner* as his love of gold was replaced by his love for Eppie. She hoped the next book Miss Eben assigned would not be so somber and moralizing.

During the second week in May, the seniors' special activities began. Senior-play rehearsals took place every afternoon, and plans for the senior picnic were posted on the bulletin board outside the principal's office.

One afternoon Tess peeked into the auditorium and watched the rehearsal taking place on the stage. The play was *The Taming of the Shrew*. Tess wondered why the senior play always had to be one of Shakespeare's, he certainly was not a favorite of hers. They had read and discussed two of his plays in English class, *Macbeth* and *Hamlet*. Wordy things, those plays; sometimes she couldn't make head or tail of them unless she read them aloud. Surely something modern would be better for high school actors.

This time next year when she was a senior, she was going to put in a word for a simpler play, she thought. But that was foolish, who would listen to Tess Trumper, the tombstone girl?—as some of the boys at Monroe Avenue school teasingly used to call her. She remembered, however, that she had put a stop to that by walloping one of them in a most unladylike manner.

She closed the door on the players and climbed the stairs to deposit her books in her locker. She stood there a moment, listening to the singing coming from Room 224. The chorus was rehearsing for the spring concert next week.

Only this morning Donna had heard her humming and had asked why she wasn't in chorus. Well, why wasn't she? She loved to sing with the Washingtons. Stella and Irene often praised her voice. She felt sure Miss Anderson, the music teacher, would have taken her if she had just tried out last fall. But there was always so much to do at Willow Hill; she had not wanted to take the time after school for rehearsals. But wouldn't joining the group have been a good way to make friends as Stella was urging? Next fall she *would* try out; it might be fun.

She shut her locker and left, humming "Santa Lucia" along with the chorus.

At home she found Seth sitting on the front steps, reading a book.

"I came over to borrow your yesterday's newspaper," he told her, slipping a marker in his book.

"I have today's right here," Tess replied. "Come on in. I'll get you yesterday's."

Seth followed her inside to the kitchen where she got the newspaper from beside Uncle Will's rocker near the window and handed it to him. She removed her hat as Seth spread the paper on the oilcloth-covered table and turned the pages slowly, scanning headlines in search of a current event for class.

Tess washed her hands, got out a loaf of bread, and cut two slices.

"Hey, Tess, the circus is coming to town June second," the boy said excitedly.

"Well I hardly think that's the sort of current event Miss Jackson has in mind."

"Say, what about this? Listen." Seth read aloud:

New Name for Organization

"A new name has been chosen in New York for the National Negro Committee. Henceforth it is to be called the National Association for the Advancement of Colored People. The committee was formed last year during the hundreth anniversary celebration of Lincoln's birth. The purposes of the organization as stated are: to promote equality of rights and eradicate caste or race prejudice among the citizens of United States; to advance the interest of colored citizens; to secure for them impartial suffrage; and to increase their opportunities for securing justice in the courts, education for their children, employment according to their ability, and complete equality before the law."

Seth looked up at Tess thoughtfully. "Do you think it would be all right for me to read that at school?"

"Of course. That's important news not just for colored folks, but for everyone." Tess spread the bread slices with butter. "Any organization that's going to work for all those things is bound to have an uplifting effect on the whole country. I especially liked that 'education for their children' bit. Have you made up your mind about school next fall?"

Seth folded the paper and took the slice of bread Tess held out. "Thanks. Judge Milburn asked me to come to his house, so I did last Saturday when I was in town and he gave me this book to read. You know, Tess, the judge is a very smart old man. I know he wants me to go to school rather than to work at the hotel; but instead of preaching at me, he gave me this book."

Tess glanced at the book. "So—he's letting *Up from Slavery* do his preaching for him, is he? And it's written by a Washington at that."

"Uh huh. It's an autobiography of Booker T. Washington. He tells about how he fought his way out of slavery to be a teacher and then how he started a school for Negroes in Alabama." Seth took a bite of bread and chewed thoughtfully.

"Well, has the book given you any ideas you can apply to yourself?" Tess sat at the table and ate her bread and butter.

Seth swallowed and looked across at her solemnly. "I don't know. I sure would like working at the hotel. Tess, have you ever seen those red suits the bellboys wear?"

Tess nodded. "But Seth, don't you think it might be better to brighten up your mind than your body? Suits wear out, but when you dress up your mind with knowledge, it's there to stay for a lifetime."

Seth grinned at her. "My, my, Tessie, you're getting to sound 'most like the old folks."

"Well, I am getting on. Irene and I will be seventeen this summer."

"I know. And I'll be fourteen in August. Do you think I'd like it there at high school?" he asked slowly, then added, "How many colored kids go there?"

Tess thought a moment. "About five I think."

"That's not very many."

"All the more reason you should add to the number."

Seth was thoughtful. "Linc is coming out to supper tomorrow night, it's his evening off. I have a hunch Irene asked him out to talk to me about school. I met him at church. He seems real nice. *He* went to high school you know."

"Yes. Irene has bragged about his education often enough, I should know."

"Reverend Harrison told Mama that he's going to ask Linc to teach us boys' Sunday-school class. The reverend has been teaching us, but he needs to be free for other things. Hope

Linc will do it. I bet he'd be interesting and could make those old Bible words sing out." Seth put the last bite in his mouth and picked up the newspaper and book. "You finished with this paper?"

Tess nodded and followed him to the door. "Tell Irene to come over. I haven't seen her since a week ago yesterday."

"She's been making over a dress from one Mrs. Converse gave her. She looks real nice in it."

"Irene would look pretty in a gunny sack," Tess stated with a short laugh. "I suppose she's hurrying to get the dress finished so she can wear it tomorrow night."

"I reckon so."

"Well, I might just drop over to your house myself tomorrow night. I've got to meet this wonderful Lincoln Johnson."

After Seth had gone, she changed her dress and cleaned the chapel. The Curtis baby's funeral was to be held there tomorrow. She supposed John Bixby would be the undertaker in charge, since he had the only baby's hearse in town. It was a small vehicle, painted entirely white and was drawn by two white ponies. When this little hearse led a procession of carriages through the streets there was scarcely a dry eye among onlookers on the sidewalks and at the windows. It cost extra for the use of the miniature white equipment, but bereaved parents usually thought it money well spent.

The chapel in good order, Tess took the clippers and rake to Judge Milburn's lot. She worked on it every day, wanting to make sure the judge got his money's worth.

She had started a savings account at the First National Bank with the twelve dollars he had given her. She wished she knew how to earn more money, enough to build a greenhouse, but a thing like that could only be a dream.

She went down to the river bank, dug up a clump of violets, and transplanted them on Baby Claude's grave, near the small headstone. The stone had a tiny bird and squirrel perched on top and the words below were:

BABY CLAUDE

FEBRUARY 14, 1870 – AUGUST 19, 1870

FOR OUR DARLING

Tess crumbled the soil around the violets. Baby Claude was six months old when he died, she thought. He probably died of what people called summer complaint, a name applied to the illness that took so many babies during Indiana's blistering summer days. How the judge and his wife must have grieved over the loss of this first child. And then there was little Alice over there, only seven when she died, and little Andrew at age three. These little ones must have been happy when their mother joined them in 1900, she thought.

She got up from her knees. Maybe she would phone the judge and see what he thought about her putting an ever-blooming rose bush there by Mrs. Milburn's stone. Should she, or should she just go ahead and do it? If the judge trusted her, why shouldn't she trust herself. She would phone the greenhouse and price rose bushes.

She took her spade and returned to the river bank for another clump of violets. This one she put on Baby Teddy's grave in the potter's field. She mustn't neglect him just because he had no one to pay for his care. Baby Teddy had been special to her and Irene for many years, ever since his parents had buried him quickly and moved on in their rickety wagon. Tess didn't even know his last name; his mother had told Mama that his name was Teddy, that was all.

Returning home, she paused just below the summit of the hill and looked up at the long, drooping willow branches swaying gently in the late-afternoon sun.

If she were smart enough, she thought, she would like to make a poem about those old willow trees. She was sure Mama could have if she had tried. Sometimes she felt stifled by all that was within her, emotions crying out for expression and for which she had no words. There was a similarity in the way she felt about the willows and her feeling toward Irene. But when she tried to express either vocally, the words slipped away, leaving a pain in her chest at her own exasperating inadequacy. Did other people suffer from their inability to express themselves? What were people really like inside? Probably not anything like the faces they showed the world. Now who would ever think that a down-to-earth, forthright person like herself longed to write poetry about wind-swept willow trees and deep friendship?

The rattle of a wagon brought her back to her surroundings. It was Peter Madison's wagon, hauling in a new stone. The wagon stopped at the Snyder lot. She hurried down, wondering what epitaph had been chosen for Otto Snyder.

"Say, Pete, that's some fancy stone you got there," she said as Peter Madison wrapped the reins around the whip socket.

"It is for a fact," Mr. Madison agreed, getting down.

"How's your wife, Ambrose?" Tess inquired of the wiry little old man still on the wagon seat.

"Oh, tol'able, Tessie, just tol'able considering all she's been through." Ambrose jumped over the wheel and joined Mr. Madison at the wagon's tail gate.

Tess stepped closer and read the inscription on the tombstone:

OTTO SNYDER

FEBRUARY 1870 – APRIL 1910

DUTIFUL SON – LOVING FATHER

"Hmmm," Tess mused. "From this it seems he wasn't much of a husband."

Mr. Madison laughed. "Well, that's what old lady Snyder ordered put on it. And I do mean ordered. What a tartar she is! Don't see how that daughter-in-law has stood it all these years, because Otto was just like his mother, high and mighty and as overbearing as they come."

"Guess she *couldn't* stand it. She's been living at the hotel since her husband died," Tess informed them.

"You don't say!" Ambrose exclaimed as he tightened the ropes around the stone to lower it. "I hear she acted mighty peculiar at the funeral."

"She sure did," Tess agreed.

"Well, if you ask me," Mr. Madison said, "there's more amiss there than meets the eye. Here, Tess, give us a hand, take this rope."

The three were silent as they eased the big stone down on the broad planks leaning against the wagon. Tess stayed until it was in place, then turned to go.

"Thanks for the help, Tess," Mr. Madison said. "How's Irene these days? I don't see you girls as often as I used to. But, I suppose, now that you're grown up you've got younger men on your mind; no time for old codgers like Ambrose and me."

"Oh, Irene's fine, works every day. I expect I'll be dropping in at the works more often as soon as school is out."

"You do that. You may find our place more interesting come June. Got a young cousin, a second cousin, coming from Muncie to learn the monument business."

"Yes? What's his name?" Tess asked.

"Jeff Madison."

Tess said the name over to herself as she walked home. That name sounded as though it should belong to a big man. It might be interesting to have a *young* man employed at the "Works." Yes, sir, it just might. She must start dropping in there oftener, as she and Irene used to.

The next evening after supper when the dishes were put away, Tess announced, "I'm going over to Irene's, Uncle Will. That Lincoln Johnson is there and I want to meet him."

"So, little Irene has got herself a beau. My, my, how the years march on," Uncle Will mused. "Seems only yesterday that I was shooing you two out of the way when I had a big crowd at a burial. You little imps felt you had to see everything. Do Stella and Sam approve of this fellow?"

"I guess so. He's going to their church now. But I'm not sure *I* approve of him. Irene's different somehow since he came on the scene." Tess frowned as she rolled down her sleeves.

"That's only natural, Tessie. And it won't be long until some fine young man will come along and change life for you too." Uncle Will put a lamp on the table and lit it.

"Not on your tintype, Uncle Will. I'm going to be an old maid and run a greenhouse."

"Time will tell." Uncle Will chuckled as he sat down with his newspaper.

At the Washingtons', Tess found Stella and Sam sitting on their front porch and the young ones playing "run sheep run" in the gathering dusk.

"Where's Irene?" she asked as she sat on the step at Stella's feet.

"She and Linc are doing the dishes," Stella answered, her rocking chair giving out with rhythmic squeaks as her heavy body moved it back and forth.

"Yes," Sam put in with a deep laugh, "and it's taking them a right long spell of time to finish up too."

"Think I should go in?" Tess asked. "I do want to meet him."

"Sure, honey, go on in. Irene wants you to know him," Stella answered.

Tess opened the front screen and entered the dark hall. A light shone across the floor from the open kitchen door at the rear. She heard the chink of china and a rattle of pans above the hum of talk in the background.

She stood in the doorway a moment before the two standing at the table noticed her. Linc was a slender young man, she noted at first glance, his lean dark face was strongly featured with a firm jaw and deep-set eyes.

"Tessie!" Irene exclaimed, looking up from the dishpan. "I didn't hear you come in. Linc this is my friend, Tess Trumper," she introduced the two.

"How do you do." Linc smiled as he nodded his head. "I've heard a lot about you."

"All good, I hope." Tess laughed, liking his smile, and thinking that his gentle mouth tempered the severity of his prominent jaw.

"Well, from what I've heard from the Washingtons, there's an angel flying around out here at Willow Hill and her name is Tess Trumper," Linc said, his smile broadening into a grin.

"Don't you believe it. I'm more likely to be the one with horns; if I had wings, I'm sure my feet would drag."

Tess got another dish towel from a drawer and helped Linc dry the dishes. He asked her what subjects she was taking.

When she mentioned that they had recently studied *Silas Marner* in English class, Linc praised the book, called it a fine example of redemption treated realistically by a great writer. Tess did not voice her own opinion of the book. Maybe, she thought, she had missed something. It might be a good idea to read it again since Linc spoke well of it.

As the conversation progressed, Tess began to understand why Irene was attracted to this young man. He was assured without being bold, humble without being servile, polite without being suave. Prepared to disapprove of him, Tess found herself liking him very much. Maybe he was worthy of Irene after all.

When the dishes were finished, they joined the others on the porch. Three-year-old Johnny was asleep on his father's lap. Danny sat on the top step, leaning his head against his mother's knee. Seth left the game and dropped down by Danny.

"What an unusually warm night for May," Linc said. "It's more like June. When's your school out, Seth?"

"Just got one more week."

"What are you going to do during the summer?" Linc asked.

"If I decide not to go to high school I can have a permanent job at the hotel. I'd be a bellboy. A red uniform goes with the job too."

"So? And what do you plan to do when you are too old to be a bell*boy?*" Linc questioned.

Stella stopped rocking to listen. Tess was sure Irene had put Linc up to this line of questioning.

",Well, gee—! I hadn't thought about that," Seth replied.

"You'll be a man before you know it, Seth, and ready for a man-size job." Linc turned to Sam. "Are you in favor of him going to high school, Mr. Washington?"

"I am for a fact. Don't know as I can send all the young

ones, but with a little scrimping, Seth can go." Sam shifted
the sleeping Johnny on his lap.

"That newspaper clipping you were showing me at supper,
Seth, the one about the Negro organization. Well, if that group
is to succeed, it's going to need a lot of educated Negroes. It's
going to need you. Who knows, if you get an education you
might be able to do something real big in the world. The Lord
has given you a good mind. It wouldn't seem right to waste
His gift."

Irene and Linc walked partway home with Tess, as far as
the potter's field. Here she insisted that they not go farther.

"You're not afraid to be alone in a cemetery at night?" Linc
asked.

"Goodness no! There's nothing to fear from the dead." Tess
laughed. "It's the live ones you have to look out for. I'm sure
the streets in town are much more dangerous than the roads
through Willow Hill."

Walking on home alone, Tess wondered if Linc's words
would have the desired effect on Seth. Perhaps what Linc *was*
would be even more persuasive than what he said. She knew
that education was having a tough battle with the red, brass-
buttoned uniform in Seth's mind.

The cemetery was especially beautiful tonight, she thought,
as she neared home. She felt reassured about Irene now that
she had met Linc. If Irene had to have a beau, this one seemed
all right.

What about herself? Would there ever be any young man
calling at her house; anyone coming to take supper with her
and Uncle Will? If there ever was such a one, might he not be
scared off by her indifferent cooking? Maybe she should ex-
periment on a cake again or even try to bake some biscuits.

6. Decoration Day

Decoration Day came on Monday. School had been out for more than a week. Tess had spent a large part of that week working in the potter's field. She wasn't going to have her poor folk look neglected on the cemetery's big day. She mowed the grass, clipped close around the wooden markers, and loosened the soil about the plants she had set out.

The cemetery was a busy place the evening of the twenty-ninth of May; people brought flowers after the sun went down so they would be fresh next day. Tess and Uncle Will gave help when it was asked for, supplying a shovel or rake or a can in which to carry water from the pump.

By nine o'clock the people were gone, leaving behind the fresh flowers to remind the world next day that their dead were not forgotten. That night Tess set her alarm clock for five-thirty so she could put bouquets out early for Mama and Papa. She wanted their flowers to be the freshest in the cemetery.

At ten minutes to six next morning, she pushed a wheelbarrow loaded with a bucket of water, garden tools, and a great bunch of pink and white peonies picked from the bushes in their yard.

She hummed softly as she poured water into the cans she had set into the ground at the head of each grave. She divided the peonies into two bouquets and arranged them in the sunken cans. She took the clippers and cut a few long spears of grass growing close to the headstones.

Standing off a way, she surveyed the lot critically. "Well, Jimpson and Agnes, I think your place looks quite presentable, if I do say so as I shouldn't," she said aloud. "Your flowers are the freshest on Willow Hill today."

She dropped the clippers in the wheelbarrow and walked on up to the willows, where she could see the graveyard on all sides. How lovely it looked, she thought, the grass so green and flowers everywhere. She sat on the A B C stone and sniffed the fragrance from the peony bush, heavy with red flowers. The bush had timed its blooming just right.

An oriole flashed its bright wings through the willow branches, a crow cawed raucously in the distance, a meadow lark trilled, and bees buzzed over the bright peonies. Tess gave a deep sigh of contentment. What a morning! What a morning! It was good to be here alone with the quiet ones. In a few hours the roads would be crowded with buggies and people swarming all over. The paraders would march out here from town and then there would be speeches and flags put on the graves of soldiers. For a few hours Willow Hill would belong to the town. But right now it belonged to her.

Would she be sitting on this stone this time next year? She would be through school and ready for a job of some kind. She should be earning her own way by then. But doing what? She'd just die, or at least want to, if she had to clerk in a store, standing behind a counter every day being polite to customers. And as for sitting at a typewriter in an office—well, she'd hate that too. If she were smart and could go to college, she might teach school, but that also was confining. She didn't mind hard work, but oh, she did want to be free! Free to run up or down Willow Hill whenever she liked; to hum, to talk to herself, to tend flowers, and to dig in the dirt.

"Tess Trumper, you are as crazy as a bedbug!" she muttered to herself.

Hearing footsteps on the gravel, she stood up and watched a woman approach with a basket of flowers. Recognizing the woman, Tess walked down to meet her.

"Good morning, Miss Anderson," she greeted the high school music teacher. "You're out kind of early, aren't you?"

"Good morning, Teresa. Yes, I caught the first streetcar out. I picked these flowers from my garden this morning. My, everything looks nice," Miss Anderson said admiringly.

"You'll need some water for those," Tess said. "I have some in a bucket down there. I'll get it."

"Oh, thank you. I'll go on to our lot. It's down on the other side."

"Yes, I know. Your mother, father, and three brothers are there," Tess said as she started toward the Trumper lot where she had left the wheelbarrow.

She returned with the water, finding the teacher arranging her flowers.

"You must know this cemetery very well, Teresa," Miss Anderson remarked, stooping to tuck a flower in at the side.

"I should. I've lived here since I was four."

"Isn't it rather lonely for you at times?" the teacher asked.

"Oh, no. We have neighbors, the Washingtons who live about a mile away."

"But that's not like living in town with neighbors right next door," the teacher said.

"Well, no. But you have to remember all these folks." Tess laughed and indicated the cemetery with a sweep of her hand.

"They are very good neighbors and not one of them has ever snooped into our affairs or borrowed a cup of sugar, and they let me do all the talking."

Miss Anderson smiled. "How did you like our spring concert?" she asked.

"I—I—I didn't go," Tess stammered, slightly embarrassed.

"Shame on you, Teresa. Is that the way to encourage our singers?"

"Well, it's a long ride into town and I'm pretty busy out here when I get home from school," Tess excused herself.

"Maybe you should be in chorus. Do you like to sing?"

"Yes, I enjoy it. I often sing with the Washingtons. I'm not as good as they are, but in a group I guess my voice would do."

"I'll expect to see you at chorus tryouts in the fall." Miss Anderson straightened from her bent position and looked up the hill. "What a beautiful sight, those willow trees. You must be very fond of them." She took a handkerchief from her pocketbook and wiped her hands.

"Yes. I think they are the best part of the whole cemetery."

"Last Christmas vacation I visited my sister in New York," Miss Anderson said. "She took me to a performance of Shakespeare's play, *Othello*. In it there is such a lovely song about willows. Desdemona sings it. I remember I looked up the words in the play as soon as I got home." Miss Anderson hummed a few bars.

Tess listened attentively. "That's a lovely tune. I didn't know Shakespeare knew about willows."

"Shakespeare knew a great many things: music, the law, art, politics, history, the Bible," Miss Anderson enumerated. "It's no wonder we quote him so often. So much of what he wrote applies to the present, no matter what the year."

"Can you remember any of the words of the Willow Song?" Tess asked.

"Just a couple of lines at the end." Miss Anderson sang:

" 'Sing willow, willow, willow;
Sing all a green willow must be my garland.'

But you can find the whole thing in the play *Othello* if you are interested."

Tess walked with the music teacher, got the wheelbarrow from where she had left it, and pushed it to the house. She went on to the cemetery gate with Miss Anderson. The teacher gone, Tess returned to the house slowly. Next time she was in town she'd look up that song at the library. Imagine, Shakespeare writing about willows way back there in the ancient times!

At half-past ten, Tess went to Four Corners to wait for the parade. The Washingtons were there as well as many others who lived at the edge of town. Stella had pushed their well-worn gocart near the curb so baby Rachel could see. The other children sat on the curb, hopping up frequently to look up the street for the first glimpse of the marchers.

"Do you have the day off?" Tess asked Irene.

"Yes. The housecleaning is finished. Mrs. Converse doesn't need me every week now."

"Say, that's too bad. You won't be seeing Linc so often, will you?"

Irene smiled self-consciously. "I'll see him at church on Sundays and at prayer meeting, and maybe at choir practice if he decides to join the choir. He has a good voice."

"Listen! I hear the band," Seth called out.

The children stepped out in the street to look. "It's coming!" Nat shouted.

"Get back here this minute," Stella scolded.

The parade was headed by a contingent of police, followed by the Soldiers' Home Band, next came a big hay wagon decorated in red, white, and blue bunting. White-frocked girls sat around the edge, hanging their feet down. Then came Judge Milburn, looking fine in his blue, colonel's uniform, as he sat erect on a high-stepping white horse. He was followed by other Civil War soldiers riding in carriages, most of them being too old to walk the distance from town.

Judge Milburn looked down at the Washingtons. Seth raised his hand in greeting. The judge smiled at him and saluted.

"Doesn't the judge look grand?" Seth said to Tess.

"He sure does," she answered. She hoped the judge would be pleased with the way she had fixed up his lot.

Boys, riding decorated bicycles, brought up the rear of the parade. The crowd scattered.

"How about seeing you at the river under our sycamore tree this afternoon?" Tess said to Irene.

"All right. About three?"

"Uh huh."

By noon the ceremony in the cemetery was over and most of the people had gone home. Later in the afternoon the place would be crowded again. It was customary to visit Willow Hill on Decoration Day.

Tess cleaned up the kitchen after dinner, then went out and sat in the front porch hammock, slowly pushing herself back and forth with her feet. People were already walking through the cemetery, pausing now and then to admire flowers and to read inscriptions.

It was warm, Tess grew drowsy. She pulled her feet up and

lay back in the hammock. Reaching out for the rope tied to the railing, she closed her eyes and pulled gently on the rope. The hammock swayed slowly again.

The summer stretched out before her like a warm, sun-drenched road, three months of it. What would she do with all that time? Irene would probably have other jobs in town or have to help Stella wash and iron at home. Mud-pie days were over for her and Irene, that was certain. It was a satisfaction to be grown up at last, but there were times when she wished for one of the old days in which nothing was expected of her but to play on Willow Hill with Irene all day and come inside only at mealtime.

How safe she used to feel on summer evenings, with Mama and Uncle Will sitting on the porch and she and Irene running about the tombstones, catching lightning bugs to put in milk bottles. Then Sam would come for Irene and they would empty the bottles and watch the fireflies spread their wings and fly back to twinkle on and off over Willow Hill. Sometimes Sam would take a chair and visit with Mama and Uncle Will before taking Irene home pickaback.

Dear Sam and Stella, what fine people they were. Salt of the earth, Uncle Will said. Next Thursday the Wallace and Hagenback circus was coming to Allerton. She must ask Irene what time they were driving in to see the parade. She had never missed seeing a circus parade with the Washingtons. When Mama was alive, both of them had crowded in with the big family and had ridden gaily into town. Circus day was wonderful! One might not have the money to see the show, but the parade was free for all to watch and admire.

The rope dropped from her hand, the hammock swayed slower and slower. Tess dropped to sleep.

"Tess Trumper, wake up!" Irene stood above her. "I waited

for you at the sycamore and here you are sleeping as soundly as Baby Rachel."

Tess sat up. "Oh, I'm sorry. What time is it?"

Irene opened the screen door and looked at the living-room clock. "Seventeen after three."

Tess got out of the hammock and smoothed her hair in the back. "Want to walk to the river?"

"Let's do."

As they climbed the hill Tess noticed the visitors, some sauntering along the main roads and bypaths, some seated on decorative iron benches on their lots and looking off into space contemplatively. Thinking about their departed ones, Tess imagined.

"Oh, look, Irene, there at the Snyder lot. That's Ottilee and her grandmother. I wonder if they are pleased with the new stone. They haven't been out since Pete and Ambrose set it up."

Irene glanced interestedly at the two in black. "I pass their house on my way to the Converses'. They have a beautiful garden. What pretty red hair the girl has."

"You should see her with her hat off. Irene, do you suppose I could fix my hair like hers?"

"How does she fix it? I can't tell from under the hat."

"Oh, all fluffy around her face, kind of puffed out and a knot in the back. Sometimes she wears a big bow of ribbon across the back too."

Irene looked at the braid wound tightly about Tess's head. "You might if you did the front of your hair up on kid curlers the night before."

"Well, that's out. I'd never go to all that bother. Who could sleep in kid curlers? It would be downright torture."

Ottilee saw Tess and lifted a hand in greeting. Tess waved back. The elder Mrs. Snyder looked up and eyed Irene and Tess sharply.

"Whew!" Irene exclaimed as they proceeded. "That old lady's got the evil eye for sure. I wouldn't want to work for her."

There was no one in the potter's field as the girls walked through to the river.

"Judge Milburn rode over to our house this morning," Irene said as they sat down on the broad rock under the sycamore tree they affectionately called "ours."

"He did? What for?"

"He came to offer Seth a job. He says his housekeeper is getting old and needs help. He'd like for Seth to move in and stay there. That way he can be nearer school and be on hand to do heavy chores for Mrs. Crawford. I guess she's been his housekeeper for twenty years or more. The judge says she's got bad rheumatism."

Tess drew up her knees and rested her chin on them. "Is Seth going to do it?"

"I think so. The judge was mighty convincing, looking so fine in his uniform. He let Seth ride his horse around the barn lot and told him that exercising the horse would be part of Seth's job." Irene picked up a stone and skipped it out over the water. "You know, I just thought of something. I've often waited in the judge's house while Mrs. Crawford collected their washing. He has a fine library. All the walls in one room are covered with bookshelves. I've looked at the books and they are mostly law books. Now wouldn't it be fine if Seth would turn out to be a lawyer? And he just might, exposed to all those books and with the judge to encourage him."

"It sure would," Tess agreed. "Just imagine going into town and seeing painted on an office door: SETH WASHINGTON, ATTORNEY AT LAW."

Irene nodded. "Yes. That's the sort of thing we have to do, Linc says, more of our people doing jobs that require brains.

But first we have to get more education to train our minds."

Tess grew thoughtful. "Well, not all people, *either* white or black, take to schooling, no matter what their opportunities. Me, for instance, I could go to school till the cows come home and I'd still not be smart enough to be called educated."

"Oh, Tessie, don't run yourself down!" Irene exclaimed.

"One of the quotations we had to learn from Shakespeare last year began, 'This above all, to thine own self be true,' well, that's what I try to do, not to kid me about myself."

"There, see how smart you are! You can quote Shakespeare."

Tess laughed. "You know, the high school music teacher was out here early this morning. She told me that there is a song about willows in one of Shakespeare's plays. I'm going to look it up the next time I go to the library."

A twig snapped up on the bank. Tess looked around. "There comes Linc," she told her companion.

Irene sat up straighter as the young man approached.

"Your mother told me where to find you," he said to Irene. "Hello, Tess. Irene, your mother said this spot was where you two often played as children." He looked out across the river. "Hmmm, this is nice."

"Sit down," Irene invited.

Tess smiled up at Linc. "We're fond of this sycamore. We once had a swing here, years ago. This place is almost as special to us as the willows on top of the hill. Irene did you ever tell Linc about our A B C stone up there?"

"No."

"Well, tell me," Linc said, dropping down between the girls. "That sounds curious."

Irene described the stone and how Tess's mother had used it advantageously.

"Did you have this morning off too?" she asked.

"No, only this afternoon. I just rode out on the streetcar on the chance you might be at home and want to take a walk."

"Irene," Tess spoke up. "Why don't you take him up to the willows so he can see for himself where you and I started our education?"

Tess watched them leave. Standing up, she could see them saunter across the potter's field and up the hill. A deep pain of loneliness crept over her as she observed Linc reach out to take Irene's hand.

Tess turned back to the river, picked up a rock, and flung it into the water with all the vigor of her right arm.

7. Circus Parade

"Uncle Will, why don't you go in town with us and see the circus parade?" Tess asked at breakfast on Thursday.

"Can't. Got a burial at eleven. The deceased lived in Kokomo and the family's bringing him here to be buried beside his wife. It's Everett Harding."

"Oh, yes, I know. His wife, Esther, lies just beyond Mama. I'm glad they didn't decide to bury him in Kokomo. Esther and several children have been waiting there a long time for him." Tess stirred her coffee. "Want me to fry you another egg?"

"No. I've had plenty. What time will you be back? In time for dinner?" Uncle Will asked.

"I don't know. But I'll fix you a snack just in case I don't." Tess drank the rest of her coffee. "You know how the Washingtons usually drive over to Grandma Barker's before they come home. If we get over there fast enough after the parade passes downtown, why we can see it again as it goes back to the circus grounds. Stella's mother lives not far from the east edge of town."

Uncle Will nodded. "Stella's younger sister and brother still live with her?"

"Uh huh. Irene says she doesn't think they will ever marry now, they're so old. Aunt Susan must be thirty-five or so and Uncle Del is almost that." Tess began stacking the dishes.

"Does Del still work at the glass factory?"

"I guess so. Aunt Susan quit her job there some time ago. Stella said she likes doing housework better, more variety to it. I wonder if they'll have their hamburger stand going today," Tess mused, taking the dishpan from its nail in the pantry.

"I shouldn't wonder. I remember Sam saying they usually did pretty well with it on circus day."

Nine o'clock found Tess at Four Corners, waiting for the Washingtons to drive by. Others were there to catch the streetcar to town. Tess sat on a bench in front of the Monument Works. She could hear the buzz of machinery inside. Evidently Pete Madison hadn't closed for circus day. He and Ambrose were too old, she supposed, to care about a circus. She hoped she never got too old to enjoy the thrill of it.

The streetcar came in sight, rounded the circle, and stopped. A man with a suitcase got off. Those waiting got on. The conductor waved to Tess as he jumped back up the step and rang the bell for the motorman to proceed. The car jangled back along Main Street.

The passenger who had just got off looked around hesitantly as though he was unfamiliar with the neighborhood. Tess watched him. His glance fell on the sign above her head and he walked toward her.

He was tall, she noted, maybe six feet one or two; he was fairly young, perhaps twenty or so, and he was as handsome as one of the moving-picture actors she had seen at the nickelodeon downtown. Without so much as a glance her way, he walked through the open door of the "Works."

Cautiously Tess turned and looked through the window behind her. The young man had set down his suitcase and was shaking hands with Pete. Maybe that was Pete's second cousin from Muncie, she thought.

"Yoo hoo! Tessie! Come on, get in!"

Tess hopped up and ran to the curb. The Washingtons' wagon was so full of scrubbed, dressed-up children, it didn't seem there was room for one more. Stella was beside Sam with the baby on her lap, the others sat on planks put across in the back. Tess squeezed in between Seth and Nat and took Danny on her lap. Irene held Johnny.

Sam slapped the reins on Zeke's back and the mule clattered off at a good clip.

"Guess Zeke knows it's circus day, Sam," Tess said. "I've never known him to be in this much of a hurry."

"He'd better get along if he knows what's good for him," Sam returned.

"Can we see the parade twice, Papa?" Naomi asked, smoothing down the skirt of her crisply starched dress.

"I aim for us to if I can find a place yon side of downtown to hitch. Then as soon as we see the parade at Third and Main we can hightail it back to the wagon and drive over to your grandma's in time to see it going back to the circus grounds."

"Grandma sure is lucky to live so near the circus," Ruth said, fingering the blue ribbon bow in her hair.

"Ruthie, that bow is going to come off if you don't stop fooling with it," Irene warned.

Main Street was noisy with the clatter of hoofs; buggies, carriages and wagons rolled along, bringing countryfolk to town for the big day.

Tess gave Danny a little hug. "Excited about the parade?" she asked in his ear.

"Uh huh. Papa told me he carried water for the elephants once when he was a boy," Danny told her. "Wish I could do that."

"Maybe you can when you're older." Tess knew she was as

excited as Danny. It seemed to her that even the air was different on circus day. The light breeze on her face seemed to whisper of strange animals, bright spangles, and band music.

"Did Irene tell you about my new job with the judge?" Seth asked.

"Yes. When do you start?"

"Next Monday. He says he's got a lot of yard work he wants done now. I won't start staying there nights, though, until school starts," Seth answered.

"Stella, I expect you'll miss Seth, won't you?" Tess remarked.

Stella looked back. "I sure will, but it will be fine for Seth. Staying with the judge, he'll learn how to live nice while he's getting an education."

"Why, Stella, there's nothing wrong with the way you live," Tess objected.

Stella nodded. "I know, but still, if Seth's going to get on in the world he's got to learn nice manners and the judge will be a fine example for him."

Sam turned off Main Street at Fifth and found a place to hitch Zeke beyond Al Hibbler's feed store on East Third. The children hopped down and Stella assigned the little ones to Irene, Seth, and Tess. They were to hold hands and not let loose for a minute or they would get lost in the crowd.

Tess held seven-year-old Naomi's hand as they walked toward the courthouse square to find a place along the curb to watch the parade. The sidewalks were crowded, everyone trying to edge out toward the street. Tess held Naomi's hand tightly and elbowed her way through so the little girl could stand at the front.

"There, how's that? Can you see?"

"Uh huh." Naomi's large dark eyes were wide with excitement.

A balloon man went by in the street with a great bunch of balloons of various colors above his head. "You can't see the parade without a balloon. Buy the little one a balloon!" he yelled in a loud nasal voice.

Another hawker went by selling whips: red ones, green ones, and blue.

A little boy standing next to Naomi let loose his balloon and cried loudly as it sailed up and blew away. His mother gave him a shake, saying if he didn't hush she'd take him home this minute and he couldn't see the parade. The threat was effective, but Tess doubted if wild horses could have driven the woman herself from this vantage point.

A policeman walked along in the street, pushing the crowd back on the sidewalk. "You've got to stay out of the way of the horses and elephants," he told the children. "Get back up on the curb."

Naomi looked up at Tess. "Do you suppose it'll ever come?"

"Sure it will. Listen, isn't that the band?"

"Sounds like it." Naomi jumped up and down and peered up the street. "I see it! I see it! It's coming!

"It's coming! The parade's coming!" came from many lips as the blasts of brass horns and the thumps of the bass drum floated over downtown Allerton, filling the air with raucous, spine-tingling, nothing-like-it, circus music.

Tess stood behind Naomi, keeping her hands on the child's shoulders. The everyday world Tess knew slipped away as the sparkling, gaudy, exciting procession passed before her.

The splendor of the women on horseback was unbelievable. Some, mounted side saddle, wore riding habits covered in colored sequins that flashed and glittered in the bright sun, making the spectators blink their fascinated eyes. The men's costumes were no less dazzling. Another brass band came along in a red wagon trimmed in gold, pulled by four gray horses. In the cages that followed, there were lions pacing back and forth, monkeys swinging on bars, a hippopotamus lying imobile in a shallow pool of water, black panthers snarling at their bars, and then came the glassed-in snake wagon with a beautifully costumed lady sitting in the midst of her slithering charges. Tess shuddered as the woman held up a wriggling creature. Oh, how could she?

Clowns in ridiculous costumes were everywhere, their faces painted in queer designs, their crazy antics bringing loud laughter from the sidelines along the line of march.

The camels, their heads held haughtily in the air, padded by, looking as though they considered the Allerton folk a contemptuous lot indeed!

Naomi shrank back against Tess. The elephants were coming! The great pachyderms, each with his trunk holding the tail of the one in front, swung along, the huge feet making a sliding, swishing sound on the brick street. Tess gazed up at the beautifully costumed ladies riding in the little houses on top. They had to hold tightly to the sides to accommodate themselves to the rolling sway of the enormous animals.

After the elephants came the cowgirls, cowboys, and Indians. Tess envied the cowgirls. Wearing divided skirts, they sat astride with easy grace, seeming almost a part of their mounts. One broad-shouldered cowboy reminded her of that young man she had seen get off the streetcar this morning, only this cowboy's face was more tanned.

As in all circus parades, the calliope came last, sending loud, harsh music over the courthouse square as spurts of steam shot up from its pipes. Tess could see a man in a red, gold-braided coat sitting inside, playing the tune on a keyboard. Finishing "Oh, Susannah," he began "On the Banks of the Wabash."

The calliope passed them, Naomi took Tess's hand. "Can we see it again, Tess, can we?"

"If we hurry." Tess clasped the little hand tightly and stepped off the curb into the street where the going was not so crowded.

All accounted for at the wagon, Sam slapped Zeke with the reins and they rolled away along East Third, across the C. & O. Railroad tracks into East Allerton.

They arrived at Stella's mother's little brown house, well ahead of the returning parade. What a crowd at Grandma Barker's; on circus day every one of her children and grandchildren visited her. Tess knew them all, for she had been here on many other circus days. In fact, Grandma Barker had once said, "I declare, Tessie, I forget you're white most of the time."

The hamburger stand had been set up in the front yard and already Aunt Susan was frying the sizzling meat on the gasoline stove at the back of the tent and Grandma was slitting buns. Customers stood at the front counter waiting hungrily to set their teeth into the onion, pickle, meat, and bun concoctions being prepared.

Tess lined up with the others on the grassy strip between the cinder sidewalk and the dusty street. There was no pavement in East Allerton. By the time the parade reached here on its return to the grounds, the circus people had discarded their set smiles and theatrical posturing. They looked tired, Tess thought, and the grand ladies seemed sort of old too. She wondered if maybe some of the color in their cheeks was painted on.

A long picnic table was set up in Grandma's back yard and baskets were unpacked. Grandma's daughters and daughters-in-law had brought food for a picnic dinner. Everyone was especially hungry, appetites being whetted by the smell of Aunt Susan's hamburgers out front.

Tess thought she had never tasted anything so good as Stella's fried chicken and Aunt Belinda's potato salad. Plates in hand, she and Irene sat on a bench under the grape arbor. The big yard was crowded and noisy.

"Shall we walk on out to the circus grounds when we finish?" Irene asked.

"Let's do."

The older children had already bolted down their food and had run along to the circus grounds. By the time Tess and Irene started, the sidewalk was crowded with people going for the two o'clock performance. Audiences always arrived early to see the side show and to spend time in the animal tent before going into the big top.

The last house and cinder walk behind them, the girls stepped into the grassy field known always as the circus grounds. Before them were the tents that had mushroomed up in the early-morning hours.

"Circuses must have some kind of magic," Tess remarked, lifting her skirt to keep it off the trampled grass. "I don't see how they get set up so quickly. Just think, this time tomorrow this whole shebang will be set up in another town."

"Just lots of people working together, I suppose, and each one knowing his job," Irene said.

All kinds of stands lined the way, with men yelling their wares; pink lemonade, peanuts, cotton candy, hamburgers, balloons, whips, and Cracker Jack.

A stream of people were lined up in front of the ticket wagon and many were already entering the main entrance leading into the animal tent from which they would go directly into the big top where the performance would take place.

"Remember that one time Uncle Will took you and me to see the *show?* Was that the summer we were eleven or twelve?" Irene asked.

"When we were eleven, because Mama was still alive then. Wish I could take Seth and all the other children to the show today," Tess remarked.

"Oh, they had the parade," Irene said, "that'll keep them playing circus for weeks. Let's look at the pictures outside the side show."

Huge posters along one of the smaller tents depicted the many sights to be seen within.

"Ten cents, one tenth of a dollar!" cried the dapper little derby-hatted man on the high platform. "Step right this way and get your tickets. Plenty of time to see the wonders here before the big show. See Elmo, the dog-faced boy! He barks, he growls, he's alive! See the Waldini midget family! They have appeared before the crowned heads of Europe! See Jaronto the sword swallower! You won't believe your eyes! Watch the flames go down the throat of our fire eater, the great Montross. Right this way for your tickets!"

Irene sighed. "Wish we could see the side show."

"Seeing the pictures is enough," Tess said as they wandered by looking up at the big pictures. "Look at the size of the giant! Now that's the size husband I should look for. He's bound to be taller than I."

After taking in all the free sights, the girls walked back to Grandma's. Stella was in the hamburger stand, helping Aunt Susan get ready for the going-home crowd. A few of Grandma's descendants had left, the others sat on the porch and in the yard. Children chased one another all over the place.

"Irene, I think I'll walk on back downtown. I want to go to the library," Tess said at the gate.

"But where shall we pick you up?"

"Don't bother with me. I'll go home on the streetcar." Tess stepped to the front of the stand. "I'm going along now, Stella.

Want to stop at the library. It's been a wonderful day. Thanks for taking me into your family again."

Stella put down the onion she was slicing and came to the counter. "You *are* part of our family, Tessie. You got carfare home?"

Tess nodded, smiled, then walked with Irene to the porch to tell Grandma good-by. The old lady rocked contentedly, happy to be surrounded by her own.

"I'm going now, Grandma," Tess told her. "I've had such a good time."

"Tessie, we're proud to have you." The old woman stopped rocking. "You always seem like one of Stella's. Law me, I've know'd you since you was a little bitty thing. How's your uncle?"

"Pretty good. He doesn't complain." Tess turned to go. "Good-by."

Walking along East Third Street toward the business district, Tess glanced interestedly at the people on the porches. What would it be like to live so close to neighbors? In this section of town some houses were neat, with fences and well-kept yards, others were rickety and neglected. Once Stella had said jokingly that she had married Sam to get out of East Allerton.

It *was* kind of a dingy section, Tess thought. Many of the inhabitants had moved to Allerton to work in the town's many factories. The neighborhood included Italians, Irish, Negroes, Polish, Welsh, and Germans. Most of them were good, American citizens. But, as Stella said, there were always a few trashy ones, white as well as Negro, who gave the neighborhood a bad name. Tess was glad the Washingtons didn't live here.

She passed the Bethel Baptist Church, which the Washingtons attended regularly. Tess had gone there with them a few times on special occasions like Children's Day when one of the Washingtons was going to speak a piece or take some part in a program.

Across the C. & O. tracks she stepped onto the paved sidewalk, stomping her feet to clear her shoes of East Allerton dust. Two more blocks and she was downtown. The parade watchers gone, the courthouse square was quiet and deserted. She stopped to look in some of the department-store windows.

At Seventh and Harmon she climbed the steps of the public library, cool and quiet inside. Tess walked across the tile floor on tiptoe, stopping in front of the charging desk.

"Will you please show me where to find Shakespeare's plays?" she softly asked the lady in charge.

The librarian nodded and left the desk enclosure by a swinging wooden gate at the back. Tess went around and followed her into the book stacks.

"There they are." The librarian pointed to the shelf. "Any special one?"

"Yes. *Othello.*"

The woman took down a book and handed it to Tess. "It will be in this volume called *Shakespeare's Tragedies.*"

Tess took the book into the reading room and sat at a table. She found the play, then began skimming the pages to find the willow song. It eluded her. Impatiently she flipped the pages again.

Doggone it! Was she going to have to read all of this blamed thing to find it? She took her library card from her purse and went to the charging desk, where the librarian stamped the date on Tess's card and on the book card, writing Tess's number on the latter.

Tess looked at the big clock opposite the desk. Almost four; there was not time to look at magazines. She must get along home to fix Uncle Will's supper. One pickup meal a day was enough for him to put up with.

Outside she walked along Seventh to Main and waited for the Willow Hill streetcar, *Shakespeare's Tragedies* under her arm.

8. Sing All a Green Willow

When Tess got off the streetcar at the end of the line she glanced at the Madison Monument Works. The door was shut and the blinds down. Pete must have closed early. Maybe he was taking his cousin to the circus tonight, she surmised. Of course that fellow might not be the cousin he had mentioned, but who else could it be? What excuse could she make for going over there? she wondered as she hurried down the road to Willow Hill.

It rained the next day. Tess watched a funeral procession drive in at half-past two. She always felt sorry for folk who had to see their dead buried in the rain.

After the burial Uncle Will returned to change his wet clothes. Seeing Tess in the hammock reading, he asked, "Well, did you find whatever it is you were looking for in that book?"

"Not yet. Guess I'm going to have to read the whole play to find it. It was tough going at first, but now I'm sort of getting the hang of it." Tess closed the book, keeping a finger in her place. "It's easier to read one of these when you don't have to. Did you ever read any Shakespeare, Uncle Will?"

"Law no, Tessie! I guess your old uncle is as ignorant as they come. Your mother was the educated one in our family. I reckon she could read Shakespeare or anything else with the best of them."

Tess nodded. "I guess I'm not much like her."

"Oh, I wouldn't say that. You got lots of spunk and determination. Yes, Tessie, I'd say you are a lot like Agnes." Uncle Will went in the house.

The rain continued to rattle down on the porch roof as Tess reopened her book and became involved again with the hateful Iago, the jealous Othello, and the beautiful Desdemona. What havoc jealousy could cause in people's lives, she thought. Recalling Miss Anderson's words, "So much of what he wrote applies to the present, no matter what the year." Tess was on the alert, trying to spot such timeless truths.

She paused in her reading and placed a finger on a phrase. These were apt words, she thought. "How poor are they that have not patience! What wound did ever heal but by degrees?"

She'd try to remember that when she became exasperated, waiting for something big to happen in her life. She looked out from the porch at the expanse of tombstones beyond. Living here, would anything exciting ever happen to her? Probably not, unless she did something about it.

She picked up a scrap of paper from the floor and put it in the book as a marker. In the morning she would make her one baking achievement, ginger cookies, and then she'd take some to Pete and Ambrose at the "Works." Meeting Pete's cousin just might be exciting. Yes sir, if she didn't act, no new experiences were ever going to come her way. She sat up in the hammock and thought a moment. Didn't she learn a quotation in Miss Eben's class that said, "If it were done, then it were well it were done quickly," or something like that. Of course, as she remembered it, that character was talking about a murder and she was thinking about getting acquainted with a young man.

She stood up and a slight smile spread across her mouth as she thought, Tess Trumper, if you aren't getting high-powered, quoting Shakespeare to yourself. Next thing you know, you'll be writing poetry!

She went inside to start supper.

Next morning there was mowing to be done on the west slope, so Tess didn't get at her cookie baking until ten-thirty. At noon Uncle Will pronounced the cookies delicious.

"When I get cleaned up, I'm going to take some to Pete and Ambrose," Tess told her uncle.

"You tell Pete that last stone he put up settled a mite too much after yesterday's rain. I think he better reset it," Uncle Will said as he left by the kitchen door.

The dishes taken care of, Tess brought in the big, galvanized washtub from the back porch and put it on the kitchen floor. She locked the doors and dipped hot water from the reservoir, at the side of the stove, into the tub. She removed her clothes, got into the tub, and scrubbed herself thoroughly with a rough washcloth lathered with a scented cake of soap.

Upstairs, dressed in clean underclothes and starched petticoats, she unbraided her hair, brushed and rebraided it, and pinned it back again in a circle around her head. She shook a little talcum powder onto a small, chamois skin and rubbed it on her face, shiny from its recent scrubbing.

She put on her good, low-cut, buttoned shoes, using the pearl-handled buttonhook Uncle Will had given her last Christmas. She slipped a pink chambray dress over her head, fastened it, and straightened the white collar and cuffs. She was not displeased by what she saw in the mirror. There was just one thing wrong—her hair! It just wasn't stylish. Hardly anyone wore it like this. It was the style to have it curly and fluffy about the face and over the ears. And here she was with a tight braid and all of her ears showing. Maybe she *should* buy some kid curlers.

In the kitchen she made a grocery list, wrapped some cookies in a clean towel, dropped them in the big market basket, and then was off to Four Corners.

Tess found the front room at the Monument Works deserted. From the back came the sound of metal applied to granite. She stepped into the big workroom. Pete saw her and put down his chisel and hammer.

"Well, if it isn't Tessie!" he exclaimed.

"I baked some cookies, Pete. Thought you and Ambrose might like some," she said, glancing around. No one else was in sight except Ambrose. Had she gone to all this bother for nothing? she thought exasperatedly.

"That's right neighborly of you. Tess has brought us some cookies, Ambrose. Call Jeff inside."

Tess relaxed. So—he was here, Jeff Madison. She put the cookies on the table in the corner. Ambrose called out at the back door and Jeff came in.

He looked different in overalls and a long, blue denim apron that reached from his shoulders to his ankles. His hair was brown and she thought his eyes were gray, but she couldn't be sure.

"Tessie, I want you to know my kinfolk, Jeff Madison. Jeff, this is Tess Trumper who lives at Willow Hill. Ambrose and I have known her since she was just a little tike."

"Pleased to make your acquaintance," the young man said stiffly.

"Hello," Tess returned, thinking that his voice didn't sound very friendly. "I saw you arrive on circus day," she went on. "I guess you didn't get to see the parade."

"No."

Pete unwrapped the cookies. "Have one, Jeff? Tess makes good cookies."

The young man took one and bit into it. "They are good. Thanks very much." He turned and walked toward the back door.

Now this was a fine thing, Tess thought, after all the trouble she had gone to to meet him, and here he was walking away.

"It was a fine parade," she put in hurriedly.

Jeff turned at the door. "Yes. The circus was in Muncie last week. I saw it there." He looked at Tess a moment, took another bite, and left abruptly.

Tess hoped her face didn't show her disappointment. She picked up her market basket. "Well, I must get along to the grocery," she said.

Ambrose helped himself to another cookie. "Best ginger cookies I ever tasted, Tessie," he told her.

"Pete, is your cousin staying with you?" Tess asked.

"Yes, he is. You see, I'd never laid eyes on him before till day 'fore yesterday. His pa, Jake Madison, and me are cousins. Grew up together as kids, then his family moved to Virginia and I lost track of 'em. They just recently moved to Muncie and Jake wrote me about Jeff wanting to learn a trade. He's a real ambitious boy. I'm glad to have him."

He may be ambitious, Tess thought, as she crossed the street to the grocery, but friendly he is not! She just as well have worn her work clothes and let her braid hang down her back. He was as cold as one of Pete's gravestones. Maybe if she had done her hair differently—!

The groceries put away in the kitchen, she suddenly remembered that she had forgotten to tell Pete about the stone Uncle Will said needed resetting. Tessie, my girl, she told herself, you better tend to your knitting and quit mooning around over Jeff

Madison. She went to the phone, turned the crank at the side, called Pete's number and gave him the message.

After supper Uncle Will sat on the porch and smoked his pipe, his feet up on the railing. The dishes put away, Tess lit a lamp in the living room, found her place in the book of tragedies, and read on. She would find that willow song or her name wasn't Tess Trumper! She was beginning to think Miss Anderson had just dreamed it.

Just as Uncle Will saw a figure turn in at the gate he heard a loud "Eureka! At last, I found it!" from the living room.

"Evening, Irene," he said as the girl mounted the steps. "Tessie's in the living room and from the sound I think she's made a big discovery."

"Good evening, Uncle Will." Irene opened the screen and went inside.

Tess glanced up. "Say, you came at exactly the right time. I've been reading like mad since Thursday evening, trying to find the Willow Song I told you about. And here it is. Sit down and I'll read it to you. Do you know the story of *Othello?*"

"No. But I expect Linc does." Irene sat in a rocker opposite.

Tess briefly told the story as far as she had read. "Now in this scene; let's see, it's Act Four, Scene Three, and Emilia, Iago's wife, is with Desdemona, Othello's wife. Desdemona says,

> *'My mother had a maid called Barbary.*
> *She was in love; and he she loved proved mad*
> *And did forsake her. She had a song of 'Willow';*
> *An old thing 'twas; but it expressed her fortune,*
> *And she died singing it. That song to-night*
> *Will not go from my mind; I have much to do*
> *But to go hang my head all at one side*
> *And sing it like poor Barbary. . . .'*

You know, Irene." Tess looked at her friend. "That's so true; sometimes a tune keeps singing in a person's head till you think you'll go crazy with the monotony of it. Ever happen to you like that?"

Irene nodded. "Lots of times. I've been humming 'Banks of the Wabash' ever since the calliope played it Thursday."

Tess returned to the book. "Well, here Desdemona sings the song. Listen.

'The poor soul sat sighing by a sycamore tree,
Sing all a green willow;
Her hand on her bosom, her head on her knee,
Sing willow, willow, willow.
The fresh streams ran by her and murmured her moans;
Sing willow, willow, willow;
Her salt tears fell from her and soft'ned the stones
Sing willow, willow, willow;
Sing all a green willow must be my garland.'"

Tess looked up from the book. "Isn't that lovely? Can't you just see 'the poor soul' sitting under our sycamore by the river, looking up at the willows on the hilltop and singing her heart out over her lost love?"

Irene nodded. "Didn't you say Miss Anderson hummed the tune?"

"Yes, she did. Let's see, it was in a minor key kind of like this." Tess hummed.

"Hmmm. Pretty." Irene pulled her chair beside Tess. "Let's try to sing the words to it." Irene looked at the book over Tess's shoulder. They sang the words haltingly, Irene trying to follow Tess's tune. After four renditions Uncle Will came in and stared at them.

"If you girls don't watch out you're going to sing that thing to death," he said with pretended harshness.

"But isn't it pretty, Uncle Will? So sad and mournful it makes me want to cry," Tess said.

"Let's sing it again," Irene said. "I think I almost know it by heart."

Uncle Will laughed. "Would you mind waiting till I'm gone? Think I'll walk over to the Corners and get a can of tobacco. I've had about all the willows I can stomach for one night."

The girls giggled as Uncle Will went to the kitchen. They heard him knock the ashes from his pipe in the coal bucket, then slam the back screen door as he went out.

Uncle Will smiled to himself as he got to the road, remembering the two faces in the lamp glow, one dark, one light, and both brightened by the enjoyment of one another's company. He wished Agnes could see them. She would be pleased to know what kind of girls they had grown to be. He put his hands in his pockets, puckered his lips and whistled a tune, unaware that he was whistling the Willow Song.

Next day Uncle Will went to church with Tess. From their pew on the far side, Tess watched Mrs. Madison and Pete come in accompanied by the taciturn Jeff. She nudged Uncle Will and whispered, "That's Pete's cousin I told you about."

Uncle Will looked and nodded, picked up a song book, and turned to the hymn the minister had just announced.

Outside, after church, Pete introduced Jeff to Uncle Will, saying, "Will Bagley runs our cemetery, Jeff, with Tess's expert help, of course." Pete winked at Tess.

Jeff nodded in Tess's direction and shook Uncle Will's hand. Tess made polite remarks to Mrs. Madison, thinking at the same time that Jeff paid no more attention to her in her white Sunday dress than he had when she wore the pink chambray.

She made up her mind that she was definitely going to buy kid curlers next time she went to town.

That afternoon she took the funny paper to the Washingtons'. She and Irene one-fingered the Willow Song on the old organ in the parlor and sang it for Stella.

"That's a mighty mournful tune," Stella remarked, humming a few bars. "It sounds real old-timey."

"It is," Tess said. "I found it in the play *Othello* and I guess Shakespeare wrote it sometime in the early sixteen hundreds."

"For mercy sakes!" Stella sat in a rocking chair and fanned herself with her apron.

"Stella, if I buy some material will you help me cut out a dress?" Tess asked.

"You know I will. What kind of dress you aiming to make?" Stella dropped her apron and rested her hands on the arms of the rocking chair.

"Oh, something summery. I was thinking of buying Suesine silk. It's that real soft stuff, you know, lightweight and washable. It's not as expensive as regular silk. I think it's around fifty cents a yard." Tess looked at Irene. "What color should I get 'Rene?"

Irene got up from the organ stool and gave Tess's face a long look. "You have been going out in the sun without a hat so often you are almost as brown as I am. Mama, don't you think yellow would be nice for her with that tan?"

"'Spect it would," Stella agreed.

"I've been sort of thinking of pink," Tess said slowly.

"Oh, you and your pink!" Irene exclaimed. "You've got pink dresses galore!"

Tess grinned. "I know. I love that color. I think, if I ever get to Heaven, I'm going to sit around for ten centuries or so in pink dresses. And I'll have a different one for every day."

"Irene, why don't you and Tess look through those *Ladies'*
Home Journals Mrs. Converse gave you. There are some summer patterns in one of them. You might find one you like,
Tess." Stella got to her feet. "I think I put those magazines in
the corner of the pantry after the girls took out the pages of
paper dolls. Come on, we'll get them."

On her way home Tess stopped at the willows and sat on
the A B C stone to look further at the three magazines she had
chosen to bring home. There was a certain pattern on the page
captioned "The American Girl's Summer Dress—For Morning
and Afternoon Wear." The dress she liked had three ruffles
which began at the knees and reached down to the ankles
and the sleeves had ruffles just below the elbows. Very narrow
ribbon was woven in and out of the lace beading around the
neck, the same at the elbows and about the waistline.

Should she get pink material and use white velvet baby
ribbon at those points, or, follow Irene's suggestion and get
yellow material and use narrow black velvet ribbon?

That might be very striking, yellow and black. How pretty
the girls looked on this page and they all had curly, fluffy hair.
She just had to change her hairdo. Maybe Irene could help
her. Let's see, she thought, how much material did that pattern
take; nine and three quarter yards of twenty-seven-inch material. Well, with her height it would probably take at least
eleven.

She turned to the beginning of the magazine and noted the
stories and articles she wanted to read. But first she must finish
Othello. She had left Desdemona last night singing the Willow
Song. She had to find out if Iago accomplished all the meanness
he had planned. What a villain that character was. How could
Shakespeare make up such a variety of people?

She wished now she had gone to see the senior play, *The*

Taming of the Shrew. Maybe when she went back to the library she would get the volume of Shakespeare's comedies and read it. There must be something to Shakespeare's stuff, since it had lasted so long and people like Miss Eben and Miss Anderson set such store by it.

It was better though, she thought, to read it on one's own instead of tearing it apart in English class for every shred of meaning. But then maybe some people would never know about Shakespeare if teachers didn't introduce him in class. Teachers certainly had a tremendous task, trying to plant seeds of culture in the minds of indifferent students like herself.

She wondered if Jeff Madison knew Shakespeare. Probably she would never find out, for at this point she didn't see how she was going to get better acquainted with him.

The sun was going down. She must get along home to prepare supper. What a perfect June day up here; the air warm, the grass green, and the willow trees trembling lightly in the summer breeze.

"*Sing willow, willow, willow;*
Sing all a green willow must be my garland."

Tess sang softly as she went down the hill, the magazines tucked under her arm.

9. Murder?

On Tuesday, Tess drew six dollars from the bank to pay for the dress material, eleven yards of pale-yellow Suesine silk. She found that it was 47½ cents a yard, eleven yards costing $5.23. There was enough money left for the pattern, the black velvet ribbon, thread, hooks and eyes, *and* a packet of kid curlers from the ten-cent store. It was nice not to have to ask Uncle Will for the money. She wished she could earn some more so that this withdrawal might be replaced.

Wednesday afternoon she took the material and pattern to the Washingtons'. Stella was ironing in the kitchen, with Baby Rachel asleep on the cot in the corner. Irene was in town working for Mrs. Converse, Stella told her. The other children were outside playing, Seth, of course, was at his new job.

"How does Seth like working for the judge?" Tess asked as she spread the yellow material on the big table.

Stella laughed. "Law me, the way that boy talks you'd think the sun rises and sets in the judge. He's sure being mighty nice to our boy. He's already got Seth reading some of his books. Just living there is going to be a real education for Seth, let alone him going to high school in the fall. Sam and I are real proud of him."

Stella put the iron she was using back on the stove to heat

and got the scissors from the sewing machine in the bedroom. She and Tess studied the directions, then pinned the tissue-paper pattern to the material. Under Stella's watchful eye, Tess did the cutting.

"This goods is going to be hard to work with, honey," Stella said, holding a piece between her fingers. "It's so flimsy, you might have done better with gingham or linen."

"Oh, but Stella, it's so soft and—and dainty. It'll be cool too. And I'm glad I got yellow."

"Well, if you get into trouble let us know," Stella replied, having had previous experiences with Tess's sewing sprees. "Remember, you must baste before you sew it on the machine."

Tess laughed. "I will. I learned that lesson the last time."

That evening instead of being on the front porch with Uncle Will, Tess sat inside by the lamp and basted. She would like to start on the machine stitching in the morning, but she'd have to do some cemetery work first. She'd set her alarm clock for six.

Stella was right, this Suesine silk was hard to sew. It puckered so easily. It was hot in here by the lamp too. A mosquito buzzed at her ear. She slapped at the air. The picture of herself, dainty and beautiful in the yellow dress, grew dim as she pricked her fingers and the thread knotted again and again.

At last the waist was sewed together! She held it up. Hmmm, it certainly didn't look like much at this stage with no sleeves. She picked up a sleeve, then put it down. She wouldn't start on that tonight. She always had trouble with sleeves. She folded all the pieces, put them on a dining-room chair, blew out the lamp, and went out on the porch.

"Get your sewing done?" Uncle Will asked.

"No. But I just couldn't sit still any longer. Think I'll take a run up to the willows to get the kinks out."

Uncle Will puffed on his pipe. "It's a nice night. But the paper predicts rain tomorrow. Good thing Grandma Willis was buried today."

Tess went down the steps. At the gate she heard the telephone ring followed by the bang of the screen door as Uncle Will went in to answer it.

She held up her skirt and jogged up the hill. How good to stretch her legs! Maybe she shouldn't have started that dress. Was it going to be too much for her as so many other sewing projects had been? How many times Irene or Stella had snatched her attempts from utter failure. Well, this time she would do it all by herself! She wondered if she could get it done in time for Sunday. If she could, she'd try using the kid curlers Saturday night. Maybe she should practice using them Friday.

Tess stopped near the willows and let go of her skirts. The sky was lovely tonight, so many stars and Halley's comet outshining them all. It was queer the way one got used to seeing that comet in the sky. All that to-do beforehand and now it was just taken as a matter of course.

She sat on the Langdon stone and stretched her legs out in front of her, leaning back on her hands. The leaves swished, making a sighing, whispering sound as the drooping branches swayed slowly from side to side.

Tess's thoughts rambled from Jeff Madison to the circus, to Jeff Madison, to the yellow dress, to Jeff Madison, to kid curlers, to Jeff Madison, to Judge Milburn, and back once more to Jeff Madison. Finally she gave up and concentrated on Pete's cousin entirely.

If she did get the dress done and wore it to church, he might not even be there. Maybe she should go over to the "Works" again. What excuse could she have for going? It was too soon to take more cookies. Why couldn't he be friendlier? How was she to get to know him? Maybe he just didn't like girls! Or was it that he didn't like big girls like herself? Doggone it, why was she getting herself into such a dither? This had never happened to her before.

Maybe tonight she would start reading *Romeo and Juliet* in that library book. She had heard that it was a tragic love story. If she got her mind on Juliet's love troubles, perhaps she could forget her own. Love troubles, indeed! Tess Trumper, she told herself, you are a nut of the first order!

She had been under the willows for more than half an hour when the neigh of a horse brought her back to reality.

She stood up and looked down toward the house. A horse and wagon were coming up the hill, several men with lanterns walking alongside.

What in the world was going on?

Halfway up, the wagon turned into one of the smaller roads, advanced a short distance, and stopped. The lanterns were set on the ground.

Tess took a short cut across the lots to investigate. She stood in the shadow cast by the Featherstones' mausoleum and watched. It was a relief to hear Uncle Will's voice.

"Right here, Chief Rosin," she heard him say. "This is Otto Snyder's grave."

Tess checked her impulse to step out and ask questions. Instead, she waited and watched two men take shovels and pickaxes from the wagon and start to dig. Why on earth were they digging up Otto Snyder? What was the chief of police doing here at this time of night?

The chief and Uncle Will held lanterns high to light the

grave. Uncle Will gave a few directions. The men worked silently.

Tess had never felt the least bit eerie about anything in the cemetery. She had seen caskets removed from graves before, but always in the daytime and for a good reason: to rebury the corpse in another cemetery to be beside other members of the family. But this was a different matter. Why would they exhume Otto Snyder stealthily, by night? She gave a slight shiver. It was sort of like a chapter in a book she had read when she was twelve, where Tom Sawyer and Huck Finn had watched a grave being tampered with at night. That episode had ended in murder. What possible reason could there be for this?

She heard the shovels hit the rough box and Uncle Will telling the men how to bring it up. She watched the wagon drive away, carrying the remains of the bank president.

She ran to catch up with Uncle Will. "What is it, Uncle Will? Why did they dig up Ottilee's father?"

"I wondered where you were," he replied. "Thought it wasn't like you to miss what was going on. You know as much about it as I do. I got a telephone call just as you left. It was the chief of police saying he had orders to remove the body. And he didn't tell me any more when he got here."

"But at night, Uncle Will. Why at night?"

"Didn't want to run into anyone out here who would ask questions, I suppose." Uncle Will opened the gate.

It was raining hard next morning when Tess's alarm clock went off. She wouldn't be able to mow the grass on the south slope, so she turned over and tried to go back to sleep, without success. She heard Uncle Will go downstairs, so she got up and dressed. It would have been a good morning to sleep, it was so cool and nice, the rain coming down gently, but steadily. It would probably rain all day. A good time to sew.

Uncle Will left right after breakfast. He and Sam had a grave to dig, rain or no rain. Tess tried on the waist she had basted the night before. It fitted, but it was hard to tell what it would be like when the sleeves were in. She turned to the picture of the dress in the magazine for encouragement.

In the afternoon she went to the Washingtons' to get help with the sleeves. Irene said it was no wonder they looked queer, Tess had sewed them in the wrong armholes.

While she ripped out the stitches, Tess related the strange removal of Otto Snyder's body. "Even Uncle Will doesn't know why," she told them, snipping at the threads in the sleeves.

Stella clicked her tongue. "No good can come of it. It's bad to go bothering the dead that way. Mr. Snyder was a harsh man; he foreclosed a mortgage on Uncle Caster's house there in East Allerton. It would have been easy for him to give Uncle a little more time. Uncle might have been able to meet the payments. But he lost his home and all he had put in it because he got laid off at the mill and Mr. Snyder wouldn't wait. Howsomever, Mr. Snyder's dead and should be left in peace. I wonder if the new president of the bank will be as hard on poor folks as he was."

"But a bank president has to be businesslike, Mama. After all, the money they lend belongs to other people," Irene stated.

"Yes, indeed," Tess said laughingly. "I wouldn't want the bank to be careless with my savings. I have six dollars invested there."

When the sleeves were basted in the right armholes, Tess put thread and thimble into her skirt pocket and started for the door.

"Irene, do you know how to put hair up on kid curlers?"

"I think I could do it. Want me to come over and try on you?" Irene asked.

"I'd appreciate your help. I'm not very handy with hair." Tess took her umbrella from the corner and put her hand on the screen.

Stella picked up Rachel from the floor and kissed her in the fat creases of her neck. "Law me! It's funny; white folks going to all kinds of bother to have curly hair and us colored folks doing our level best to straighten ours. Nobody's ever satisfied with what he's got. The good Lord must get tuckered out, folks being so faultfinding with what He's give us." She stroked Baby Rachel's curls lovingly. "You let us know if you hear any more about digging up Mr. Snyder's corpse."

"I will. Thanks for the help. I'll start on the skirt tomorrow. That shouldn't be as hard as the waist. But of course there is the skirt placket. Those are pretty tricky," Tess said as she left.

It had stopped raining and the cemetery was fresh and smelled of flowers and moist earth. Tess passed the Snyder lot with its gaping grave and pile of dirt. The extensive planting had been destroyed by last night's digging. When would they return the body so this place could be replanted? Tess wondered. She disliked seeing a lot remain like this for very long.

Uncle Will was on the front porch. It looked as though he were waiting for her. He waved the newspaper in his hand and Tess walked faster.

"Tessie," he called out as she opened the gate. "Look here at the headlines in today's paper I just got over at Four corners!"

Tess climbed the porch steps and took the newspaper. Big black letters blazed across the top.

WIDOW ACCUSED OF MURDER!

Quickly Tess glanced below and read,

Autopsy performed on body of bank president, Otto Snyder. Traces of arsenic found.

Last night, at the instigation of Mrs. Lathrop Snyder, an investigation was launched into the sudden death last April of her son, Otto Snyder. Traces of arsenic found in the exhumed body led to the arrest of his widow, Anna Lee Snyder, under suspicion of murder. Mrs. Lathrop Snyder swore out the warrant for her daughter-in-law's arrest.

"Now what do you think of that?" Uncle Will asked.

"Murder! Golly, Uncle Will! Why that's awful! Poor Ottilee. Do you suppose it's true, that Mrs. Snyder did poison her husband?"

"Well, whether she did or not, I'm sure she must have felt like it at times if all the tales I've heard about him were true. Nobody liked him. A lot of folks had reason to do him in, I expect."

"Remember how queer she acted at his funeral? She didn't shed a tear and the way she dropped dirt in on him, just as though she were saying, 'Good riddance,'" Tess said handing back the paper. "Will they take her to jail?"

"Yes. It says farther down in the piece that she was arrested and put in the county jail last night and without bail. I wonder what made the old lady suspicious?" Uncle Will followed Tess inside. "I wish you'd take a look at the chapel before two o'clock tomorrow. The Hanrahans want to have a service there for their little girl who passed away yesterday."

"All right. Is that the Hanrahans who bought the lot next to the Weckworths'? I believe they buried his mother there last year." Tess put her sewing on the table.

"That's the family. He owns the People's Drugstore there at Third and Main."

After supper Tess finished reading *Othello*. What a bloody ending! How dramatic to have Emilia sing "Willow, willow, willow," as she died. Shakespeare certainly knew how to wring every ounce of emotion from a situation. Poor Desdemona, the victim of Othello's jealousy, unwarranted jealousy stirred up by that hateful Iago.

What had driven Ottilee's mother to murder? That is, if she was guilty. How did Ottilee feel? Terrible, probably. Tess wondered if Ottilee and her brother would be called on to testify against their mother. What a mess for a family to be in.

She turned to *Romeo and Juliet*, read a few lines, then closed the book. Getting into one of Shakespeare's plays, she had discovered, was the hard part. She would start this tomorrow.

She picked up the lamp and started toward the kitchen for a drink of water, looking with distaste at the pile of yellow material on the sewing machine in the dining room as she passed through.

Next morning she was in the chapel by seven-thirty, wearing her old work clothes. She welcomed this clean-up job; it gave her a good excuse to avoid sewing. She was beginning to wonder if she hadn't bitten off more than she could chew. It made her a little sick, remembering the miles of ruffles she was going to have to hem before she even started ruffling them. Why hadn't she chosen a plainer pattern? With all the gores in that skirt, think of the seams to be basted! If she could just run them up on the machine without basting!

There wasn't much to do in the chapel. Since the floor didn't have to be swept, the pews weren't dusty, just a little dust on the arms at the ends. She dusted the organ, sat on the stool, pulled out the stops, pumped the pedals, and tried to pick out the willow tune.

It sounded good, she thought, even better than on the Washingtons' instrument, the organ that had been given to them long ago by the Brubakers, when the latter bought a piano.

Tess added a few chords with the left hand. She wished now that she had practiced more when Mama had tried to teach her to play. That had always been her big trouble; she had no patience with tedious, small things. Her lagging interest in making that yellow dress, she supposed, was the most recent example.

She sang as she played.

"The poor soul sat sighing by a sycamore tree,
Sing all a green willow."

She sang it once, she sang it twice! Say, Tessie my girl, she told herself, that's not half bad! She played it again and hummed.

A slight rustle in the chapel made her whirl around on the stool.

There, halfway down the aisle, stood Jeff Madison!

10. Yellow Dress—Kid Curlers

Tess jumped up, remembering in one dismayed thought that her denim skirt was soiled from kneeling to weed a flower bed before she came here, that her hair was hanging down her back in a braid, and that her face was probably dirty.

"Pete sent me over to look around," the young man stated soberly. "There wasn't anyone at the house. I heard your music here, so I came in. What was that mournful thing you were singing?"

Tess walked toward him. "It's a song I found in *Othello*. Shakespeare's *Othello*," she added, accenting the author's name. Thank goodness she had something high-powered with which to begin this conversation.

Jeff took no notice. "Is it all right for me to wander around and look at the stones? I guess Pete has made a lot of them, hasn't he?" he asked, twirling his hat in his hand.

"Oh yes, Pete's been in business here for more than twenty years." Tess stood in the aisle beside him and noted with satisfaction that she had to look up to meet his eyes. He was definitely over six feet tall, she decided. "I've been cleaning up in here for a funeral this afternoon. Would you like for me to show you around? Pete's put up some very fine monuments and headstones."

"Why yes, I would, if you have the time and it wouldn't be

too much trouble." Jeff smiled at her for the first time. "You know I can't get used to the idea of a young girl living in a cemetery. Don't you get lonely?"

Tess started up the aisle, Jeff beside her. "Not often. There's so much to do, helping Uncle Will, and, during the school year, there's scarcely enough time at all. You'd be surprised how much work there is to running a cemetery. A cemetery is one place that every family is going to do business with sooner or later. I expect I know about more families in Allerton than anyone who lives there. I see folks out here burying their dead, see them come to visit the grave often right after the burial and then less frequently as time makes them forget. But another death in the family will jog their memories and here they come again with plants and cut flowers."

They walked outside, Tess leading the way up the hill, stopping at stones and monuments she thought good examples of Pete's skill. At the top she pointed to the Langdon stone and related that Willow Hill Cemetery had started here with the burial of this family, murdered in 1842.

"Say, speaking of murder," Jeff said, looking down at the stone, "what do you know about the Snyder murder? Pete said he had put up a stone for him."

"Yes, it's over there, beyond that pile of dirt beside the open grave." Tess led the way. "Night before last the chief of police came out with two men to get the body. I watched them open the grave. It sort of made me think of the graveyard scene in the book, *Tom Sawyer*." She watched his face for a look of recognition, but there was none.

They walked to the Snyder lot where Jeff inspected Otto Snyder's stone. "That's a fine piece of granite," he said, leaning over and feeling the indentation around the lettering.

"How did you get interested in the tombstone business?" Tess asked.

Jeff straightened and set his hat forward to keep the sun out of his eyes. "We buried my sister back in Virginia and I went with Pa to buy a headstone for her. Pa told me then about this cousin of his in the business. So when we moved to Indiana and Pa thought I ought to learn a trade, why Pete just naturally came to mind."

Tess pushed away some dirt that had been tossed on top of a shrub. "Think you are going to like the monument business?"

Jeff shrugged. "Well, it beats working in the coal mines. That's what I was doing in Virginia. But I got no hankering for cemeteries, I can tell you. Gives me the shivers just to be here."

Tess looked at him in surprise. "Why, Willow Hill is beautiful! Don't you think so?" She pointed up the hill. "Just look at the willows up there. Isn't that the loveliest sight you've ever seen?"

Jeff looked at the trees disinterestedly. "They're all right I suppose. But all I can think of are the corpses under the sod. To me a cemetery is a creepy place."

Tess's eyes narrowed. "I disagree with you entirely. Death is as natural as birth. Everybody experiences both. Unless you change your outlook, I expect making tombstones is not your dish of beans."

Jeff shrugged again. "Oh, I reckon one job's as good as another. I'll make out," he said lackadaisically.

Tess searched his face. Disappointment slapped hard, like a stinging whip. No question about it, he was handsome, but the inner man did not live up to the promise of his features. Maybe she wouldn't go to all that trouble with kid curlers after all.

Tess spent the next few days hemming and gathering yards and yards of yellow ruffles. The dining-room table was covered with fluffy mounds of the yellow Suesine silk. Uncle Will said it surely was going to be *some* dress; that is, if she ever managed to get all the pieces together.

It may have been because she was so glad to stop sewing for an hour or so each day that the reading of *Romeo and Juliet* gave her such pleasure. Tired from bending over the sewing machine, she would jump up, stretch her arms over her head, grab the book, and make for the front porch and the hammock. The Montagues and the Capulets were a welcome relief from ruffles and seams. By the time she reached the last page and the last lines of the play:

> *For never was a story of more woe*
> *Than this of Juliet and her Romeo.*

the dress was still far from finished.

Otto Snyder had been back in his grave for some time before the Herlemans arrived to redo the planting on the lot. Tess, inside at the sewing machine, heard their wagon, and jumped up to the screen door to see who was coming in. She went out and walked up to the Snyder lot.

"Hello, Mr. Herleman," she greeted the florist as he removed tools from the wagon. "Hi, Andy." She nodded to his son, who was lifting down a roll of sod. "Glad you're going to fix up this place. I wanted to do something about it but Uncle Will said old lady Snyder wouldn't like it if anybody touched it but you folks."

"Good morning, Tess." Mr. Herleman leaned a shovel against a tombstone and smiled at her. "You're right. She gave us exact orders as to how she wants things."

"Willow Hill looks nice, Tess," Andy commented, looking about. "We haven't been out here for some time. Most folks come out to our greenhouse and buy plants, then do the work on their lots themselves. Yes sir, looks like you and your uncle are doing a nice job."

"Well, we've had just the right amount of rain to keep things green," Tess answered, watching the short, stocky Andy skillfully unroll the sod to cover the recently opened grave. Andy was a man now, but he hadn't seemed to grow much taller than he had been when she used to watch him helping his father as a boy. Too bad he couldn't have had some of her own "growingitis," she thought. But short or tall he knew the flower business from A to Z. She had always enjoyed talking with him and his father on their occasional visits to Willow Hill.

"Does that pretty little Negro girl still live around here?" Mr. Herleman asked. "The one I used to see playing with you?"

"You must mean Irene. Yes, the Washingtons still live over near the river. Irene works, sometimes at home, sometimes in town. We see one another often. Their oldest boy, Seth, is working for Judge Milburn and is going to high school this fall," Tess informed the Herlemans.

"Say that's fine," Andy put in. "Are you still going to high school?"

"Uh huh. Be a senior when I go back."

"Seems ages since I graduated from Allerton high. I heard they had a fine basketball team last year." Andy heaved down another roll of sod and spread it over Otto Snyder's resting place.

"I guess so. I don't know much about the team."

"No? I was on the team there at high school and I still play at the Y.M.C.A. twice a week. It's a great game."

Mr. Herleman laughed. "Andy's a basketball nut, Tessie. Thinks everybody should be as enthusiastic as he is."

"Well, if I were a boy I might like to *play* it," Tess said slowly, "but just watching others have all the fun while I sit still is not for me."

Andy was on his knees; he looked up at Tess. "Geemanetties, Tess, if you were a boy what a great center you'd be with your height. No other center would ever get the tip off on the center jump from you," he finished admiringly.

Back at her sewing, Tess slipped the yellow dress with its basted-on ruffles under the machine needle, let down the foot, started the wheel, and pedaled below, guiding the material along with both hands. How nice it would be to be a boy and not have to wear skirts! Right now, skirts were way down on her list of favorite items. She'd never again make a dress with ruffles!

On Saturday, July 2, Tess did some mowing on the north slope, pulled a few weeds on the Milburn lot, and watered the shrubs. Pushing the lawn mower with one hand, she carried the sprinkling can in the other. Near the house she met Pete Madison's wagon, Pete and Jeff on the seat.

"Morning, Pete. Hello, Jeff. Whose stone you got there, Pete?"

"It's for Mrs. Manly and her baby," Pete replied.

"Hold up a minute, Cousin Pete," Jeff requested. "I want to talk to Tess." Pete obliged and Jeff jumped down. "You can drive on, I'll be there in a minute."

Tess put down the sprinkling can as Pete said "Giddap" to his horse. Jeff sauntered toward her.

"Pete was telling me they have some real nice fireworks and

a band concert at the Soldiers' Home every Fourth of July. I was wondering if you'd like to go."

Tess's mouth dropped open in surprise. "You mean you want *me* to go with *you?*"

Jeff grinned. "That was the general idea. You do know how to get out to the Soldiers' Home, don't you?"

"Oh, sure. You ride downtown and transfer to the Soldiers' Home car." She let go of the lawn mower and looked up at him. It would be nice to be seen with the good-looking Jeff, and this would be a chance to wear the new yellow dress. But did she really want to be with him? After all he didn't like Willow Hill. What was the matter with her? Who was she to be so particular, when no young man had *ever* asked to take her out before? Jeff was tall, good-looking, and Uncle Will knew him. What more could she ask?

Jeff frowned at her hesitation. "Well, do you want to go or not?"

"Oh, well, sure, I'd like to go. What time?"

"If we start at seven, would that get us out there by eight? The concert starts then, Pete says, and the fireworks at about nine or so."

"Yes, seven would be about right."

"All right. I'll call for you then." Jeff turned and walked after Pete's wagon, already halfway up the hill.

Tess picked up the sprinkling can and pushed the lawn mower toward the house. She wondered why she didn't feel exuberant like the girls in stories when young men asked to take them for an outing. After all, why had she baked those cookies? Why had she made the yellow dress? Why the kid curlers? For Jeff, of course. If only he didn't seem so—well so blah, so sort of dull.

Tess Trumper, she told herself, don't be so picky. Who are

you to find fault, you're no great bargain yourself! Be thankful you are going to the concert and fireworks with a young man and that you have a new dress to wear!

Irene came over that evening and the two sat on the steps to exchange confidences.

"Is Linc going to take you to the band concert on the Fourth?" Tess asked.

"No. He has to work. Mrs. Converse has a houseful of guests. All Mama's folks are coming to our house to spend the afternoon and evening. You know how we can see the Soldiers' Home fireworks almost as well at our place as at the Home," Irene replied.

"Jeff Madison is taking me to the concert," Tess said matter-of-factly.

Irene slapped a mosquito on her ankle. "He is? So—he's the reason you've been making that yellow dress! Is it finished?"

"All but running the black velvet ribbon through the lace beading around the waist, sleeves, and neck. Want to see it?"

In the living room Uncle Will looked up from his newspaper. "Evening, Irene. I was just reading here about the big championship boxing bout taking place out in Reno, Nevada, Monday. That Negro boy, Jack Johnson, looks real good to me. Jim Jeffries is going to have to hump himself to knock that fellow out."

Irene nodded. "Yes. Uncle Del thinks Jack Johnson will win. Ever since he stayed 14 rounds with Tommy Burns two years ago, his championship has been disputed. But if he knocks out Jim Jeffries, why then no one can say he isn't the world's first Negro heavyweight champion."

"What does Linc say about it?" Tess asked.

Irene laughed. "Oh, you know how Linc is! He says we've

got to have Negro champions in all fields of athletics, as well as science, the arts, and education. And that when there are, then the Negro will really have arrived in this country and will be ready to take his rightful place in responsibility and leadership." Irene sobered. "Linc has awfully big ideas. Papa says if there were more young Negroes like Linc, we would really go places in the next fifty years."

"Fifty years!" Tess exploded. "Golly, 'Renie, that's ages! You and I'll be old women by then!"

"Papa says it will take fifty years or more for us to get where we're going, considering the hard way we have come and the rough road we'll have to travel."

Uncle Will nodded. "Sam Washington is a smart man; knows what he's talking about, I expect. You know, Irene, I forget you Washingtons are Negroes. Somehow you're just nice folks; good neighbors I like and respect."

Irene's white teeth flashed in a broad smile and the lamplight reflected the shine in her large dark eyes. "We love you too, Uncle Will."

Tess brought a lamp from the kitchen, lit it and started toward the stairs. "I'm going to show Irene my yellow dress."

Upstairs, Irene inspected the ruffled creation on Tess's bed. "It's beautiful, Tess. You've done a fine job. What a chore those ruffles must have been."

"I hope never to tackle another ruffle as long as I live," Tess replied. "Sit down while I run the velvet through and I'll try it on."

Irene sat on the bed; Tess pulled a chair near the lamp on the dresser. Fastening a safety pin in the end of the black velvet ribbon, she wove it in and out through the eyelets of the lace beading around the waist, sleeves, and neck. Irene helped with the bows.

The new dress on, Tess looked in the mirror, then paraded up and down, liking the swish and swirl of the ruffles about her ankles.

"It's lovely, lovely, Tess!" Irene exclaimed. "I like it on you better than pink. Your tanned face is just right with that color and your hair looks kind of gold, at least in the lamplight."

Tess put her head on one side and sent herself a broad smile in the mirror. "Well, I guess it was worth all the work. Don't think I'll wear it to church tomorrow; I'll save it for the band concert." She leaned closer to the mirror, then opened a dresser drawer and took out the packet of kid curlers. "Irene, would you show me how to do my front hair up on these? Then I can do it myself tomorrow night."

"Sure."

Tess removed the dress and hung it in the closet. Irene went downstairs and brought up a pan of water. Tess seated herself in front of the dresser and Irene took the hairpins from the tight, braided circle on top of her friend's head. Unbraiding it, she brushed the long tawny mass, covering Tess's shoulders like a rippling, golden cape.

"Oh, Tessie, you have such beautiful, long hair. Are you sure you want to frizzle it up, here in front?" Irene touched the straight strands appreciatively.

"Of course. It's so straight and plain. I'd like to look stylish for once in my life."

Irene parted off the front section with the comb and began wetting small portions, rolling them on the curlers and fastening them tightly at the scalp.

Tess surveyed herself in the mirror when the job was finished. "Golly, I look deformed with all those round knobs on the front of my head. Are you sure they have to be that tight?"

"Positive."

Tess sighed. "All right. I suppose I can stand it. But it's an awful price to pay to be beautiful." She giggled. "What a joke! It would take more than a few kid curlers to achieve that on me. I bet I won't sleep a wink."

"Well, I think your hair is beautiful straight. But I suppose you know what you want." Irene braided the back hair.

"I sure do! I want to look as beautiful as Ottilee Snyder!"

"All the trouble she's in now, I expect she'd just as soon change places with *you*," Irene said as she tied the end of the braid with a piece of string.

11. Fourth of July

Discipline and self-control kept Tess from hopping out of bed during the night to remove the knots of torture from her head. The picture of herself, a curly-haired, yellow-clad princess, walking the paths at the Soldiers' Home with the handsome Jeff, eased somewhat her periods of sleeplessness.

Rising at six on Sunday morning, she wondered if she had slept at all. It seemed as though she had tossed about all night. She twisted her braid into a knot in the back and pinned it firmly. She would wait until after breakfast to do her hair. A glance in the mirror gave her a pain in her stomach. What a scarecrow! No wonder she hadn't slept well. She had better cover her head or Uncle Will would lose his appetite. She tied a scarf over the offending wads of kid curlers and went downstairs.

During breakfast Uncle Will glanced at her covered head from time to time and controlled his tendency to smile. "I declare," he said, "I can hardly wait to see the new Tess hidden under there. I've got to tend to some things down on the east slope, but I'll sure be back in time for the unveiling."

Tess's bedroom door was closed when Uncle Will came upstairs to get ready for church. When he was dressed in a white shirt and his Sunday suit, he tapped on her door.

"Tessie, would you tie this bow tie for me?" he called. There was a pause, then the door flew open. Uncle Will gasped at the figure before him.

"Great guns, Tessie! Where on earth did you get all that hair?"

"Oh, Uncle Will isn't it awful? What'll I do with it?" There was real anguish in her voice as she stood there, her hair standing up high and bushy from her forehead like a wheat field ready for threshing. "I've brushed and brushed but it won't behave. I thought it would just curl a little." She looked back in the mirror, cocked her head on one side, wrinkled her nose in distaste, then began to laugh. "Oh, Uncle Will, did you ever see anything so funny? If the circus were in town I bet I could get a job as a freak in the side show."

Uncle Will, glad to be able to let go, joined in the laughter. "It's good to hear you laugh, Tessie. Don't think I coulda held in a minute longer. I tell you what you do, wet your comb and see if that won't tame it down a mite."

"I guess Stella knew what she was talking about when she said I should leave it straight." Tess parted the hair and was able to partially control it with the dampened comb. "Well, anyway, I can be more sympathetic with Irene and her curly-hair problems. She's told me, but this experience proves her point."

Tess was uncomfortable in church. She hadn't been able to wear a hat; it wouldn't fit over the new hairdo. The knot on her neck seemed about to fall down, though it was as full of hairpins as a porcupine was full of spines; the top felt loose and unnatural.

Coming out after church, she saw the Madisons and Jeff down on the sidewalk. Jeff was looking up at her, a frown wrinkling his face. Tess shook hands with the minister and descended the steps, feeling more self-conscious than she ever had in her life. This fancy hairdo was not for her, she decided. She felt as uncomfortable as she had the first time she put on a corset, only in reverse. The hair was as loose as the corset had been tight. Oh, the problems of fixing one's self to please a man!

Jeff came forward, still frowning. "Hello. You don't look like yourself," he said frankly. "What did you do to your hair? Hope you don't wear it that way tomorrow night."

A wave of resentment rose in Tess's throat. So—! He didn't like Willow Hill, he didn't like her hairdo, drat him! Granted, her hair had turned out a mess; still, if he were the right sort he would have been more sensitive to her feelings and not mentioned how she looked.

"Sorry you don't like it," she said, the edge in her voice denying the statement. "I curled it. A girl likes to change her hair now and then. This *is* the style now, you know," she said loftily.

"Well, it doesn't suit *you* at all. I'll walk you to the streetcar," he said, taking her arm to guide her through the crowd on the sidewalk.

She pulled away and made toward the spot where Uncle Will was talking with Pete and his wife. "You don't need to," she called over her shoulder. "Uncle Will and I usually walk home on a nice day like today." She'd show him he couldn't make slighting remarks about her hair even if he was as handsome as the hero she had seen once in a play at the Allerton Opera House. She knew she was no beauty, but when she put on that new yellow dress and tamed her hair, well, Jeff Madison just might be surprised!

Uncle Will had to step along to keep up with Tess on the eight blocks' walk to Four Corners.

That night Tess set her alarm for five. Fourth of July was
going to be a busy day, she must get an early start.

Next morning Uncle Will had just built the fire in the
kitchen stove when Tess came down.

"My, you're up early. It's only five-thirty."

"I know. I'm going to wash my hair and straighten out all
the crinkles. And you know how long it takes it to dry." Tess
measured coffee in the blue granite coffeepot, put in water from
the bucket, and set the pot on the stove. "Let's see, you have
two burials this afternoon. Either one going to use the chapel?"

"Yes. The Whitneys' married daughter is being brought from
Bluffton to be buried on their lot. They want a service in the
chapel at three."

"Well, I'll wash and dry my hair first, then I'll do the chapel."
Tess got the dishes from the cupboard.

Breakfast over and the dishes washed, she took a bucket outside and dipped water from the rain barrel at the corner of the
house. Rain water wasn't as hard as their well water, and it
left her hair so soft and shiny that it was well worth the extra
bother of straining it through a cloth to get out the bugs and
leaves usually floating on top of the rain barrel.

The water strained into another bucket, she put it on to heat
while she took a wash bench from the back porch and put it
down in the yard. Washing her long thick hair was a big job
and a splashy one. She got the special cake of Packer's Tar
soap, kept just for her hair, three heavy towels, which she hung
on the nearby clothesline, a tin cup to pour on the rinse water,
and a large washpan. Such a lot of paraphernalia and a to-do,
just because of those blamed kid curlers; her hair wasn't really
dirty, she had washed it just last week.

The hair washed, she dried the bench, pulled it into the sun,
and sat down. She held up strands of hair and fanned them

with a large palm-leaf fan. An hour and a half of sunning and fanning and it was dry enough for the sides to be pinned back out of the way.

Tess got a dishpan and went to the garden patch near the back fence to pick green beans for supper. Squatting in the bean patch she searched out the full-grown beans, leaving the small ones to mature. The hot sun on her back finished the hair drying.

Enough beans picked, she pulled the ripe tomatoes, noting that they were ripening so fast she was going to have to can some in a few days. She'd have to get exact instructions from Stella again, she didn't remember from last year.

As she hurried from one task to another, Tess felt like the Red Queen, in *Through the Looking-Glass*, who said to Alice, ". . . it takes all the running you can do to keep in the same place." She could hear the far-off bang-bang of the big firecrackers in town and was glad she didn't live in the midst of all that noisy celebration.

It was three-thirty when she put the green beans on to cook with a piece of ham, and four o'clock before she was free to take a bath. What a day! She wouldn't have long for the bath; she had asked Uncle Will to come in at five for supper so she would have time to dress and be ready when Jeff came at seven.

She took down the big washtub hanging on a nail on the back porch and set it in the kitchen. Three times she filled a bucket at the pump in the back yard and carried the water inside to the tub. A teakettle of boiling water took some of the chill off the cold well water.

Her clothes on a chair, she stepped into the tub. The cool water felt delightful to her hot feet. Getting the five feet ten inches of Tess Trumper down into a round tub, twenty-seven inches in diameter, took some doing. But Tess had grown up bathing in this very tub. She was an expert.

Sitting in the tub, her feet close to her body, her knees stuck up almost to her chin. She sloshed the water up over her shoulders and back, getting wet all over; she stood up and soaped, then sat again and rinsed. Usually she lingered over the rinsing, but not today. There wasn't even time to contemplate the chapel funeral she had just witnessed. The flowers had been so pretty too, but on this hot day they'd wilt in a hurry. She must get up there to the Whitney lot early in the morning and take care of them.

After supper Uncle Will offered to do the dishes while she prettied herself for the band concert. Tess accepted gratefully.

At six-fifteen she came out on the porch where Uncle Will sat with his feet on the porch rail, tipping back his chair. The chair came down with a bang, he took his pipe from his mouth and gave a low whistle. Tess stood in the middle of the porch and turned about slowly, a smile of satisfaction on her lips at his reaction.

"Tess Trumper, if you aren't a picture! That dress is a beauty. And please, girl, don't ever try any more flim-flams with your hair. You've got good ears. I like to see them, style or no style. That braid of yours looks kinda like a crown and, with your height, why you might be a queen of some foreign country. You sure look pretty, honey." Uncle Will stood up, knocked his pipe on the porch railing, and looked at her fondly. "Just wish Agnes could see you right this minute." He cleared his throat. "Well, I got some more work to do on those new graves. You'll probably be gone by the time I get back. Have a good time."

Tess went inside and glanced at the clock. It was six-twenty. She would have time to buff her nails some more. She started upstairs to get her nail buffer. The telephone rang and she went to the kitchen to answer.

"Willow Hill Cemetery," she said.

"Hello. Is this Tess speaking?" a low, masculine voice asked.

"Yes, this is Tess." Could this be Jeff calling to say he wasn't coming? Had her frizzly hair yesterday scared him off? And after all the pains she had gone to today too!

"This is Linc. Linc Johnson."

"Oh, hello there Linc," she replied, relieved. "Happy Fourth of July!"

Linc laughed. "Thanks, Tess. And it *is* a happy Fourth. I don't know when I've been so happy and excited. I just called the newspaper office and Jack Johnson knocked out Jim Jeffries in the Reno bout, and now, a Negro is the *uncontested* heavyweight champion of the world!" He paused. Tess could sense the exuberance in his controlled voice. "I had to tell someone. Thought of Irene right off, of course, but they don't have a telephone." He paused again "If any of the Washingtons happen to drop by, will you tell them the news?"

"I'll do better than that," Tess returned. "I'll go over there right now and tell them. All of Stella's kinfolks are there. I'll just love springing this good news on the crowd."

"It will mean a lot to everyone of them." Linc's voice grew calm. "A boxing championship wouldn't mean so much to most white folks, but to us Negroes, it means we are on our way. The day will come when we will have champions in every sport. Our people have had to work and struggle and that makes for strong bodies to take part in athletics. We'll show the world one day, and not just in the field of sports either." He laughed. "Excuse me, Tess, for being so long-winded, but I just had to talk into a sympathetic ear."

"Sure, Linc, I understand. And I'll go right over and tell the folks. Any special message for Irene?"

There was silence; then, "Tell her Mrs. Converse approved the carriage-house idea. She'll understand."

A quick glance at the clock as she went out the door told her six-twenty-five. If she hurried, she could be back by seven.

Walking up the hill quickly, yellow ruffles brushing her ankles at every step, Tess didn't know when she had felt so content with herself and the world. "Glad tidings" always exalted the bearer, she supposed.

A brisk breeze was blowing away the humidity of the hot July day. On the hilltop the willows waved their branches at Tess. Her inner eye caught a brief glimpse of a sweet-faced woman and two little girls sitting on the A B C stone. "How do you like my yellow dress, Agnes?" she asked softly. The willow branches swayed with a whispering rustle. She gave a skip, and the yellow ruffles swirled out as she lifted her head and sang under her breath,

"Sing willow, willow, willow . . ."

Even before she came in sight of the Washingtons' house, Tess could smell coffee and the tantalizing aroma of sizzling fish. She knew it was fish, for Grandma Barker loved them and Sam always managed to go fishing just before the old lady was expected. The appetizing odors reminded Tess that she had scarcely eaten any supper at all, she had been in such a hurry to get at her dressing.

Approaching the gate, she took in the sight before her. Two long tables, planks on sawhorses, stretched out under the trees on one side of the front yard. The tables were loaded with food and, sitting at the tables on benches, heavy planks on nail kegs, were the numerous Washingtons and Barkers. Grandma sat at the head of one table, Aunt Susan beside her busily picking the bones from the old lady's fish.

Children were everywhere, food in their hands, not bothering to sit at the tables; there was so much for city children to see and do out here at Aunt Stella's and Uncle Sam's.

On the other side of the yard, Stella and several other women were busy at the fire where coffee boiled in big cans and fish fried in huge iron skillets set up on iron gratings over the fire.

Tess paused at the gate and wished she had some relatives; uncles, aunts, cousins, grandparents. When these children grew older they would have wonderful memories that she would never know, memories of a close-knit family in which every member was interested in the doings of all.

Stella was the first to spot Tess at the gate. She smiled broadly and turned over her place at a skillet to a sister-in-law. Wiping her perspiring face on her apron, she hurried forward.

"Tessie, Tessie! If you don't look grand!" She opened the gate and Tess stepped in. "Turn yourself around and let me have a look at you." She put her hands on her hips and took in the yellow dress.

"Stella, I didn't come over to show off. I've got news, news for everybody. Do you suppose you could get all the folks to listen? I'd like to tell them all."

Stella's face sobered and little wrinkles of curiosity crossed her forehead. "Why sure, honey. I'll try." She led the way to the porch and picked up a pan and a tin spoon.

Irene ran over. "Tessie, that dress is a dream, even prettier than I remembered. I'm glad you came to show me before you left. And I'm glad you fixed your hair the old way. I don't think any other way would look like you."

"How right you are," Tess said with a smile.

Irene watched her mother in surprise as Stella stood on the porch and pounded the pan with the spoon. The laughing, chattering voices stopped and all looked toward the porch at Stella, as surprised as Irene at the interruption.

"Listen, folks," Stella called out in her strong voice. "Tessie Trumper's come all the way over here to tell us something. Now you be quiet and listen, you hear?"

Tess looked down at the faces before her, faces wreathed in smiles at sight of her. She was their friend.

"I just had a telephone call from Linc Johnson," Tess said. There was a soft exclamation from Irene. "He wanted me to tell you that, in Reno, Jack Johnson knocked out Jim Jeffries, and is now undisputed heavyweight champion of the world!"

There was a brief silence, then a ripple of voices rose into a wave that crashed on shore as Uncle Del jumped up, threw his straw hat in the air and yelled,

"We got ourselves a world champion at last! Jack Arthur Johnson's done it! 'Little' Arthur's delivered us just as sure as Moses did the Israelites!"

Irene hugged Tess. Seth and the big boys leaped about in the yard. Grandma Barker jumped up, her fish forgotten, and grabbed Aunt Susan, the two of them laughing and crying.

Never had Tess seen anything like it, this unrestrained show of emotion. She tingled at the excitement. Probably never again in her lifetime would she be able to bring such joy to so many.

Aunt Susan and Grandma brought Tess to the table and set before her a plate filled with fried chicken, a crispy hot blue gill, Aunt Belinda's potato salad, baked beans, and sliced tomatoes. Stella put a cup of hot coffee beside it. They all talked to her at once, wanting to know how Linc got the news, exactly what he had said, all the details she could remember.

Tess ate and drank as though she had never heard about

supper before and talked and laughed with these warm-hearted, sincere friends. Irene sat across from her and drank in all the words about Linc. The laughter, the sudden bursts of "Hallelujah" on all sides, the spontaneous dancing around the tables in uninhibited glee; all these she was sure she would remember when she was an old lady.

Looking across at Irene, Tess remembered Linc's particular message. "Oh, Irene, I nearly forgot; Linc said to tell you that Mrs. Converse has approved the carriage-house idea, whatever that means."

Irene sat up straighter and Tess saw her eyes widen and her soft, generous mouth curve into a shy smile.

"What's that all about, honey, the carriage house?" Aunt Belinda asked.

Irene climbed over the bench. "I'd better help Mama," she said. Tess watched her take over Stella's place at the fire. Maybe when they were alone Irene would explain, she thought.

Suddenly there was a swish in the sky, then a bang! Everyone looked up. A Roman candle flamed and spurted a fountain of fire into the sky.

Tess put down her cup. Oh, my gosh! The band concert! The fireworks! And—and—Jeff! She hopped up and cried out, "Anybody know what time it is?"

Uncle Del pulled out his watch. "Fifteen after seven."

The yellow ruffles flew over the paths, through the potter's field, up to the willows and down, as though propelled by some unseen engine, as indeed they were, Tess's feet generating a speed they'd never heretofore achieved.

Breathless, she arrived at the front porch and stopped at the bottom step to look up at the glowering young man sitting there in Uncle Will's chair.

"Oh, Jeff, I'm so sorry," she said as he stood up. "I was over at the Washingtons' and there was so much excitement, I forgot all about you and the time," she explained with naïve candor.

Jeff stood up, changed the position of the elastic sleeve holders on his upper arms, straightened his bow tie, picked up his coat lying across the porch railing, and bent to retrieve his hat beside the chair, putting that natty item of straw headgear on his head with a snap that boded no good for the girl in front of him.

"Are you in the habit of forgetting dates you make with young men, Tess Trumper?" he asked angrily. "I reminded you of it again yesterday, as you well know." He pulled out his watch. "You are half an hour late!"

Jeff's anger and air of injured pride put all thought of further apology to flight. Tess, her breath recovered from the run, put her hands on her hips, Stella fashion, and looked up at him critically, a wave of sudden dislike sweeping her, head to toe.

"This is the first date I've ever had with a man, Jeff Madison," she said frankly. "And if this is the way they act when a girl is a little late, why then maybe I won't want another. I had an important telephone message to deliver to the Washingtons."

Jeff descended the steps, set his straw hat over on the side of his head at a cocky angle and looked her in the eye. "Just what could be more important than your date with me?"

"Why, I had to tell them that Jack Johnson knocked out Jim Jeffries this afternoon." Tess looked away and the memory of the pleasure she had witnessed a short time before made her expression soften. She turned back to Jeff. "Oh, you should have seen them, Jeff, all the Barkers and the Washingtons. They were just beside themselves with joy. Jack Johnson is the first Negro to win a world championship, you know."

Jeff drew his mouth into a thin line. "Well of all the—! You made me wait all this time just for that! I heard about that fight and I'll bet the whole thing was a fluke. Jack Johnson couldn't possibly have beat if the fight was on the up and up. Why, Jim Jeffries is one of the greatest fighters of all times and—he's white."

This was the last straw! All the disappointment, disapproval, and distrust of Jeff Madison that had been mounting ever since she had learned of his aversion to cemeteries, now reached the high peak of no return.

She bit her lip to control the explosion boiling inside her. Mama used to tell her that temper tantrums accomplished nothing, that angry words only generated more anger from others', and one's cause, no matter how just, suffered. At the age of eleven she hadn't understood this completely, but at this moment she knew what Mama meant.

With as calm a voice as she could manage, she said, "The Washingtons and their relatives have been my friends for years. This was important to them, a real milestone in the achievements of their race. And," she added with emphasis and a flash in her eyes, "Jack Johnson won that fight fairly; it was no fluke of luck. Linc would have told me if it had been."

Jeff put his coat on his other arm and tucked his thumbs in at the lower part of his suspenders. "Who's Linc?"

"Irene's friend who works in town. He phoned me."

"Oh, well, another black. He wouldn't be likely to tell you how the fight really went."

Tess turned away, went up two steps and looked down at him. "I guess we'd better not go to the concert. You and I don't seem to be getting on so well. I'm sorry I was late. I told you that already. So if you don't want to accept my apology and understand my reason, well—I guess that ends it."

"Oh, come down off your high horse and come on. We'll probably miss most of the concert, but we can see the fireworks."

Not once during the whole evening did Jeff mention the yellow dress. In fact, during the streetcar ride and the two hours at the Soldiers' Home, conversation was at a minimum.

When they arrived at the Home, the band, seated in the round cupolaed bandstand, set in the center of the big park, was playing the last number, Sousa's "Stars and Stripes Forever." The circles of benches around the bandstand were all taken, and the grass was crowded with hundreds of seated townsfolk, out here to enjoy the entertainment. Jeff and Tess had trouble even to find places on the grass. Tess sat on the ground with some reluctance, thinking of the yellow dress.

The beauty of the fireworks bursting into flaming splendor in the dark sky was all but lost on Tess. After all the preparation and anticipation, what a letdown! She wished she had stayed at home and watched the display with Uncle Will from the top of Willow Hill as she had other years.

Afterward, when she let herself think of this first date of hers, she remembered only one pleasant moment.

Coming home, the streetcar was so crowded that she and Jeff had to stand on the rear platform. She held onto a side rail to steady herself as the car lurched forward.

"Why, hello there, Tessie," a voice said beside her.

She looked down at the speaker. "Oh, hello, Andy."

Andy Herleman gave her a broad smile. "Nice concert, wasn't it?"

"I didn't hear much. Got there too late." She looked over Andy's head at Jeff, crowded to the other side of the platform.

"You sure have grown up, Tess," Andy said, his brown eyes

friendly and admiring. "You look as pretty as a daffodil in that dress."

"Why, thanks. I made it myself."

Andy nodded appreciatively. "How are things at Willow Hill?"

"Good, a little dry though. We need a good rain. I've had to carry water to the garden a lot lately."

"How are your tomatoes coming along?"

"A little too well. I can't find time to can them."

"Ours too. Mom's making catsup tomorrow."

This commonplace conversation restored her usual good humor. And, when she got home and discovered that the back of her yellow skirt was covered with grass stain, the remembrance that Andy had compared her to a daffodil helped her forget the fiasco of her first date.

12. A Senior

July burned on and Willow Hill began to show the ravages of no rain. Each evening Tess carried water to certain delicate plants, but it was a futile battle against the relentless sun.

Scarcely a day passed without one to three burials, many for small children and babies, the little white hearse and white ponies making many sad trips into the cemetery. "Summer complaint" was a scourge to small children.

Jeff telephoned twice to invite her out. Tess declined with careful politeness, saying there was so much work at Willow Hill that had to be done in the evenings during hot weather, that she could not go. The second invitation, to take her to the Allerton theater to see one of the plays being put on by the summer stock company, *was* a temptation. She resisted the inclination to say yes, remembering the Fourth of July. She didn't want to be a hypocrite, accepting just because of the show, when she disliked Jeff himself. With *his* good looks, he would have no trouble finding another girl, she was sure.

On a warm, moonlit night in August, up at the willows, Irene told Tess that she and Linc were going to be married in September and live in the rooms above Mrs. Converse's carriage house.

Tess had known this was inevitable, but even so, her world

at Willow Hill would never be the same without Irene. The unexpressed hope that, in Jeff Madison, she might find a friend who would understand her at least partially as well as Irene, had faded after their short acquaintance.

She and Linc, Irene said, were going to work for Mrs. Converse until they saved enough to start a business; their dream business, a delicatessen and catering service. There would come a day, Irene predicted, when Irene Johnson's nut bread would be as well known and popular in Allerton as Stella Washington's sweet rolls.

On Friday, August 19, Ottilee Snyder's mother was brought to trial and Donna Grant's mother was buried at Willow Hill. Tess wasn't sure which girl she was sorrier for.

Early the following Sunday morning, Tess went up the hill to tend the cut flowers that had been left Saturday on a new grave. She found Donna sitting on the grass beside the mound of the new grave on the Grant lot.

Tess sat beside her. "You're out here awfully early, Donna."

"I couldn't sleep, so I just slipped out of the house and caught the first streetcar." She paused. "But it doesn't help, Tess, being here, I mean. I can't find Mama out here at all. What am I going to do?"

Tess watched the girl's eyes fill with tears. "Give yourself time, Donna. You'll find her. You'll find her in some familiar place you and she knew together. Now take my mother and me, for instance. I was only twelve when she died and if it hadn't been for Stella and Irene Washington I don't know what I'd have done. I tried to find comfort at her grave, but it didn't help. It was Stella who told me that Mama wasn't there, that I'd probably find her someplace where we had had fun together. She was right; I found Mama up there by the willows. Come on, I'll show you."

She led Donna up the hill to the willow grove, explaining about the A B C stone and the pleasant experience Agnes Trumper had made of learning the alphabet for her and Irene at this place.

Donna dried her eyes. They sat on the low, flat stone, shaded from the early morning sun, already gathering momentum for another hot day.

"The awful thing is, Tess, I never told Mama how I appreciated her, and now it's too late." Donna removed her hat and laid it on the stone.

"Don't worry, she knows." Tess took some grass and wiped the dust from her work shoes. "Mama used to say that a mother's reward came when a daughter passed along what she had been taught to *her* daughter. So you see, you and I have obligations to fulfill to our mothers when we have daughters."

Donna sighed. "Oh, Tess, do you suppose we'll ever get married?"

"Pretty as you are, you're bound to."

"Well, it looked to me as though *you* weren't doing badly," Donna said, a hint of a smile appearing. "Who was that handsome fellow you were with on the Fourth at the band concert? I saw you but couldn't get close enough to speak."

"That was Jeff Madison. But we didn't get along very well. He wanted to take me out again, but it seemed a waste of time when I didn't enjoy being with him."

Donna raised her eyebrows. "Do you mean to tell me you turned him down?" Tess nodded. "Tess Trumper, what a thing to do! I wish a handsome man like that would take a shine to me. Johnny Hardy's the only one I've ever had a date with and he is such a boy. That Jeff looked real old."

"Twenty-two, I think."

"That old? Gee!" Donna picked up her hat. "Oh, Tess, here I am talking about boys and Mama just put in her grave! And I came out here to think about her. I'm just awful."

"No, you're not. You've got to go on living, and liking boys and wanting to talk about them is part of living." Tess wondered if it were true or if she were just saying the first thing that came to mind. Well, anyway, Donna was looking better; that was the important thing. It was exhilarating to have this girl need her.

Donna rose. "I must go. Papa doesn't know where I am."

"I'll walk you to the gate. Did you read about Mrs. Snyder's trial that started last Friday? Oh, but of course you didn't! That was the day—" Tess stopped, wishing she hadn't spoken of Friday.

"No, I didn't read it. That was the day Mama was buried. Poor Ottilee. What do you suppose will happen to her mother? Maybe she didn't do it. But if she didn't, who did? Mr. Snyder wouldn't take arsenic of his own accord. He was very well satisfied with himself, Papa says."

At the gate Donna turned to Tess. "Thank you, Tess. I feel a lot better. I'll probably see you again next week. Papa wants to come out and then we want to order a monument over at the Madison Works. Mama always admired the angels out here. I expect that's what we'll get her."

If all the angels at Willow Hill ever took wing, Tess thought, there would be as many as the heavenly host singing out the "Glad tidings" long ago, or as many as those climbing up and down Jacob's ladder. But if the Grants liked angels, who was she to suggest something else. "Yes, an angel would be nice," she said aloud. "And soon I'll be seeing you every day when school starts. Just think, Donna, we'll be seniors!"

On Tuesday, September 6, Tess managed to get to Four Corners early in order to catch the seven o'clock car. She wanted time to pass Judge Milburn's and walk to school with Seth. She had told Stella she would show Seth around high school, where he should go, and help him in any way she could.

Pete Madison was unlocking his front door as Tess arrived in front of the "Works."

"Morning, Tess. First day of school, I guess. Catching an earlier car, aren't you?"

"Yes. I want to get to Judge Milburn's in time to walk to school with Seth. It's his first day." Tess hoped her car arrived before Jeff came to work.

"So—one of the Washingtons is going to high school. Sam and Stella must be mighty pleased. You know it had crossed my mind to ask if Seth might not be interested in working for me and learning the trade. Sam's a good worker but can only give me part time. I could use another full-time person."

"But you have Ambrose and—and Jeff." Tess wished that car would hurry.

"Oh, I guess you haven't heard. Jeff went back to Muncie. Said the monument business wasn't for him." Pete shook his head and stood with one foot up on the doorsill. "I had high hopes for that boy at first. But he had the goldarnedest notions about a cemetery. Said it was spooky and scary. He even disliked going there in broad daylight to help me set a stone. Imagine!"

Tess laughed and relaxed now that there was no chance of Jeff appearing. "Well, it takes all kinds, Pete. I guess Willow Hill's got to be in your blood. It's a good thing Allerton has us to see to things out here. Uncle Will says that, after doctors, we and the undertakers are the most needed people in town. Everybody dies just as sure as everybody gets born."

"Right you are, Tess. Well, here's your car."

At a quarter to eight Tess stepped up on Judge Milburn's porch and rang the bell. Seth opened the door. He was dressed neatly in a dark suit, light-blue shirt, and dark tie. His black shoes gleamed with polish, his black ribbed stockings were pulled up tightly under his knee pants.

"Good morning, Seth. My, how nice you look." Tess smiled and looked into his worried eyes. She thought she knew something of his fears. She had been a scared freshman once herself. But it must be even harder for Seth, knowing there were so few Negroes in Allerton high.

"Hello, Tess. I'll get my cap."

Tess went into the hall. The judge appeared, newspaper in hand. "Good morning, Tess. Nice of you to stop by this morning. I told Seth you would. I think he's been up since daylight getting ready." He watched Seth take his cap from a chair. "Do you have your lunch and your pencils and notebook?"

"Yes sir, right here." Seth touched his pocket and held out his lunch box.

"When you get a book list we'll go downtown together and buy your books. It'll make me feel young again to be getting schoolbooks." The judge unfolded his newspaper. "Did you tell Tess the news?"

Seth rolled his cap in his hands. "Oh, no. I forgot." He turned to Tess. "Linc Johnson's in the paper this morning."

"Linc? Why, whatever for?"

The judge extended the paper to her. "It's right there on the front page."

Tess put down her lunch and took the paper. She read:

BUTLER POINTS TO NEW SUSPECT IN MURDER TRAIL

Jim Trottman, Negro, held under suspicion in murder of Otto Snyder.

Last Saturday, Lincoln Johnson, Negro butler for the socially prominent Converse family, came to the police and reported that he had witnessed Jim Trottman, the Snyders' gardener and handyman, acting strangely. According to Johnson's story, he saw the new suspect trying to dispose of an arsenic receptacle back of the Snyder barn. Trottman became sullen, then pugnacious, Johnson said, when he questioned him. Johnson thought the actions suspicious and reported them. Trottman has worked as gardener for the Snyders for the past ten months.

The trial of Mrs. Snyder, for the murder of her husband, has been in progress for two weeks. Police are still questioning the new suspect.

Tess returned the newspaper to the judge. "Could it have been this man, Judge?" She picked up her lunch.

"Couldn't say. We'll find out in court. If it turns out that he is the one, Mrs. Snyder will have Lincoln Johnson's alertness to thank for her freedom. Well, you better get along. Seth mustn't be late his first day."

"Oh, I'll never be late, Judge," Seth said earnestly.

The judge put his hand on Seth's shoulder. "I know this is a big day for you, Seth. You'll be scared and uncertain, but you can handle it. Just remember that great-grandma of yours, Rella Washington, and the courage it took for her to run to a new life here in Indiana. You've got strong blood in you, Stella's and Sam's, now see that you make the most of it."

Seth looked into the judge's eyes and seemed to absorb encouragement from the man's touch. "Yes, sir. I'll remember." He squared his shoulders, smiled, and turned to Tess. "Come on, Tess, let's get going to that high school."

Seth Washington was on his way.

All of a sudden, as the two of them mounted the school steps, Tess remembered that she was a senior. She had been thinking so hard about the problems Seth might encounter as a freshman, that, for the moment, she had forgotten her own exalted station. At last she was one of the elite, one of the group she had admired and envied for three years. She must be smarter than she thought to have arrived at this station. She lifted her head higher as Seth opened the door for her.

She took him to the freshmen assembly room and introduced him to Miss Eben, in charge of freshmen registration.

Seth, cap in hand, looked into the eyes of the English teacher and was reassured. Tess smiled at him, reassured too at the gleam in Miss Eben's eyes, knowing the teacher was seeing in Seth fresh soil for her seeds of "character development as ex-emplified in the English novel."

Down at the bulletin board, outside the principal's office, Tess joined other students, scanning the schedule sheet for the room numbers where their classes were to meet.

"Do the seniors meet in 101 the same as last year?" she asked Donna, just walking away from the board.

"Oh, hello, Tess. Yes, 101. Imagine it, you and I in the senior assembly room at last. Say, do you suppose Ottilee will be there? Did you see the morning paper? Maybe her mother didn't do it after all." Donna walked beside Tess toward 101.

"Yes, I read the paper at Judge Milburn's this morning when I went after Seth. I know Lincoln Johnson quite well. He's going to marry my best friend, Irene Washington, the girl I told you about."

"Honest to goodness, Tess, you know the most interesting people; Judge Milburn, Ottilee Snyder, and now this Lincoln Johnson!" Donna exclaimed.

"You get to know everyone when you live at the cemetery," Tess returned breezily.

At half-past three Tess waited at the front door for Seth. "Well, how did it go?" she asked when he appeared.

"Pretty good, I guess, for a first day. I'm the only Negro among the fifty-seven freshmen and it's kind of hard to be different and alone. There were quite a lot of Negroes at Monroe Avenue school. There, I never thought about it." He put on his cap as the two reached the sidewalk.

"Sure, Seth. We different ones just have to be tougher than the others. I'm a different one too, you know."

"You, Tess? But you're white."

"There are all kinds of ways of being different that make problems for folks besides color. You see, I'm taller than any other girl in school and taller than most boys too. And if you don't think that's a problem, Seth Washington, then I don't think you're as smart as I thought you were."

"Well, you're not much taller than I am, Tessie, and I'm only fourteen."

"Yes. I expect you are going to be a big man, Seth. You'll soon be ready for long pants. And, you know what? You're going to be a big man in other ways too. Someday they'll call you Lawyer Washington or maybe Doctor."

Seth's eyes shone. "Golly! You think so, Tess?"

"Bet my bottom dollar on it!"

Tess got off the streetcar at Four Corners and walked to the end of the sidewalk onto the road toward Willow Hill, her thoughts back at high school. It was good for Donna to be busy with school affairs. Soon the thirty-five seniors would organize and elect officers, and the class of 1911 would assume its earned place of leadership in Allerton high.

It might be a good thing if Donna were elected a class officer, maybe secretary or treasurer. It would help her forget her recent loss. And what about Ottilee? She certainly needed something to take her mind off her mountain of trouble.

So deep in thought was Tess that she was nearly at the gate when she stopped short and realized that something had been wrong with the familiar scenery she had just passed. She turned around and looked back.

There, across the road, on the very spot upon which she had often built her imaginary greenhouse, was a big pile of fresh dirt. She ran back along the road, crossed it, stood on the high ridge along the ditch, and looked at the site. Someone had been digging, and from the look of it, preparing a foundation for a building.

She walked home slowly, feeling as though her dream had been stuck with a pin and now hung limp and as unlovely as a child's burst circus balloon. Of course it had been an unrealistic dream, she knew; but oh, what an interesting one. She had seen herself efficiently bustling about a shining greenhouse, raising magnificent flowers, and making them into extraordinary floral pieces for Allerton funerals.

Oh, well, she still had Willow Hill and its constant need of her, she comforted herself as she went in the house.

Uncle Will came into the living room, a newspaper in hand. "Tessie, just wait till you read what's in this morning's paper. Linc Johnson—"

"Yes, I know. I read it at Judge Milburn's this morning. I want to go over and see what Irene knows about it." Tess took off her hat and dropped it on a chair. "Uncle Will, do you know who's building something across the road? You know, in that spot where I once told you I'd build a greenhouse if I could."

"Oh, yes. They started digging there this morning," her uncle answered. "You won't believe it, but that's exactly what they are building, a greenhouse!"

Tess's pricked dream balloon went even limper, wrinkled and forlorn.

"A greenhouse! But who would build a greenhouse in competition with the Herlemans?"

"Oh, there won't be any competition. The Herlemans are building it. I talked to Mr. Herleman over there at noon today. Andy's going to run this one."

"Andy! But he doesn't know enough to—"

"His pa thinks he does. And I shouldn't wonder if he's right. That boy's a worker, smart too, and strong as an ox."

Tess picked up her hat and went upstairs to change her clothes. Now she supposed she'd have to think up something else to dream about doing when she got her diploma. Andy Herleman had just shot her greenhouse dream to pieces.

13. Mortgage—a Serious Thing

The following week, under police questioning, Jim Trottman confessed to the poisoning of Otto Snyder, and Ottilee's mother was free. Irene told Tess that there were some in East Allerton who thought Linc had done wrong in giving evidence against one of his own kind.

"But Linc says no one, no matter what his color, has a right to break the law. They say though, that Jim Trottman had bad grievances against Mr. Snyder. But of course there's no excuse whatsoever for murder," Irene said.

"I expect Mrs. Snyder had bad grievances against Mr. Snyder too. Uncle Will says he was such an old devil; being his wife all those years and living in the same house with old Lady Snyder—well, I expect if I'd been in his wife's shoes, I'd have felt like putting poison in his soup long ago. Wonder what Ottilee's grandma will do now," Tess pondered.

Ottilee's grandmother did the only thing left; she took to her bed, refused to eat, died within the week, and was buried beside her son. Tess wondered what Ottilee and her mother would put on *her* stone: Gone But Not Forgotten? They'd never forget that old lady, that was sure.

On Sunday, September 25, Irene Washington was married to Lincoln Johnson. The wedding took place in the Washingtons' front yard with all the kinfolk looking on. Tess and Uncle Will were there, Pete and Ambrose and their wives.

"I watched you and that cute little Irene grow up," Ambrose had said when Tess told him Irene would like him to come to the wedding if he cared to. "I wouldn't miss that wedding. Got to check up on Linc Johnson to see if he's good enough for our little girl. But I 'spect he is. Sam seems satisfied with him, and Sam's mighty particular about his children."

Judge Milburn drove out in his carriage, bringing his housekeeper, Mrs. Crawford, and Seth.

It was a perfect day for a fall wedding, the air clear, the sun warm, the sky deep blue, and the leaves on the maple tree, under which Irene and Linc stood, had just begun to turn gold and red. Indian summer was the most beautiful time of year in which to be married, Tess decided as she watched.

To Tess, Irene seemed as perfect as the day. She was dressed in a golden-brown dress of an excellent quality silk. Irene had made it from one Mrs. Converse had given her. But today, no one could have recognized it as a made-over dress, Irene was that skillful with a needle. Tess marveled, remembering her own struggles, even with new material. The shade of the dress brought out the soft, rich brown texture of the bride's lovely face. All around the knot of hair on the back of her head, Tess had pinned tiny yellow asters from Stella's flower garden. Watching and listening as the two said their vows before Reverend Harrison, Tess thought that even expensive carnations or roses from a florist would not have been as right for Irene as those little asters.

For a moment her thoughts drifted from the wedding ceremony to the greenhouse and adjoining building going up across from Willow Hill. If she had designed them herself they couldn't have been more like her dream. But she mustn't think of that now. Irene was leaving her. Youth was galloping by like a swift horse and leaving her behind, leaving her old and alone. At least she would feel alone without Irene and certainly she *was* getting on, going on eighteen now.

As far as she could see, she would never be saying these words with a young man before a minister. The boys at school avoided her just as they had last year. No boy wanted to take out a girl he had to look up to. Be proud to be tall, Stella had said to her again and again, and to Irene, be proud to be black. Well, height might be stately and black strong, but even so, both were hard to live with at times. She must quit thinking about herself. Irene was getting married!

It was wonderfully noisy and jolly after the ceremony. Tess forgot her moments of introspection and was her usual outgoing self, laughing, talking, friendly. Once she thought of Donna; she must tell her about this tomorrow. Someday she'd bring Donna over here to meet the Washingtons, it would do her good. The Washingtons would be good for anyone, she went on thinking, there wasn't a mean bone in any of them.

Uncle Will had to leave early; a grave must be dug for a Monday-morning burial. Birth and death took priority over everything, even wedding festivities.

That evening there was a nip in the air; Tess and Uncle Will put on coats before sitting on the front porch.

"Guess our days for porch sitting are numbered," Uncle Will said, putting his feet up on the porch rail and pushing his chair onto its back legs.

Tess sighed and moved the hammock back and forth slowly. "'Spect so. I probably should take this hammock down and put it away. But I hate to, for that means the end of summer. Oh, Uncle Will, wasn't it a lovely wedding and didn't we have fun?"

"Sure did. And how many children do you suppose fell in the river? Seemed like every time I looked around, a bedraggled, dripping kid was coming around the house."

Tess laughed. "I helped three into dry clothes myself and there were several whose mothers got to them before I did. And oh, how happy Irene and Linc were. You know, Uncle Will, I have felt just awful, thinking of Irene living in town, not having her close by. But after seeing her go off with Linc in that buggy, both of them laughing at the rattling tin cans tied on behind—well, I wouldn't have it any other way."

"That's my Tess," Uncle Will said. "How are things at school?"

"All right. Johnny Hardy was elected president of the senior class and Donna is secretary. That's nice too, because Johnny took Donna out twice last spring and to the Soldiers' Home on the Fourth of July. Now that they will be at class-officers' meetings together, he may ask her out again."

"Ottilee Snyder back in school yet?"

"No. I imagine she may be there tomorrow."

"Well, she sure looked like a different girl at her grandma's burial," Uncle Will said, knocking the ashes from his pipe. "She and her mother held hands there at the graveside, and although their faces were serious, you could just feel their happiness; not at the death of the old lady of course, but because mother and daughter had found each other at last without the meanness of Otto and his mother to pester them."

Tess stopped the hammock. "Uncle Will, did I ever tell you that you are a very discerning man?"

"Discerning? Hmmm. New word. Where'd you pick that up?"

"In Miss Eben's class. You know, she and Seth are getting on very well. As his first book report last Friday, he reported on *Up from Slavery*, and if ever a book was filled with character development, it's that one. Seth said Miss Eben was pleased."

Next day Ottilee Snyder returned to school. During the morning the stares of the curious caused her to flush, making her more beautiful than before her trouble, Tess thought. As the day wore on and she attracted less attention, Ottilee relaxed and seemed to enjoy being back. Tess wondered if she and Donna should watch for her after school and tell her they were glad her mother was free. Or perhaps they shouldn't mention at all that her mother had been in jail.

After school Tess had just taken a seat in the cemetery car when Ottilee took one beside her.

"I'm going out your way," she said to Tess. "Mama's going to meet me there to choose a stone for Grandma."

"Oh," Tess said, for a moment at a loss for words. "I'm I'm sorry, Ottilee, for all the trouble you've had. More than your share, I'd say."

Ottilee gave a short sigh, then smiled wryly. "Well, Tess, there's this about it; I guess I never need worry about a summer of trouble in my life again. There never could be another summer as packed full of trouble as this one. If it hadn't been for Lincoln Johnson, poor Mama might have been convicted. He was just wonderful."

"He is a fine man. He married my best friend yesterday," Tess said.

"Married your best friend! But he's a—" Ottilee paused.

"Of course. My friend Irene is a Negro too. We grew up together. Neighbors, you know, a big friendly family. They have been so good to me."

Ottilee looked at her closely. "Tess, you are a very unusual girl. Mama will be interested to know about that wedding. She wants to do something for Lincoln Johnson. Maybe she can send them a wedding present."

"Oh, I'm sure Linc wants nothing for doing the right thing. He is a man of very high principles," Tess stated emphatically.

"I'm sure he is. Mama is planning to call on him at the end of this week. There has been so much for her to take care of since she got home, Grandma taking to her bed, then her death and funeral."

"Did your grandma—well—were things right between her and your mother before she died?" Tess asked, her curiosity getting the better of her.

"If you mean did Grandma ask Mama's forgiveness—no. But Mama had suffered so much even before going to jail, that she forgave Grandma anyway, saying that some folk just are the way they are and circumstances will never change them. Papa was like that too." Ottilee looked out the window on the opposite side of the streetcar.

"And what about Jim Trottman. Did you ever suspect him?" Tess asked.

"No. He was a very good workman. I never dreamed he had a grudge against Papa. But of course I didn't know what had gone on down at the bank. He held Papa responsible for the bank's foreclosure on a mortgage on his little house there in East Allerton. And, knowing Papa, I expect he *was* responsible for Jim losing his house. Papa was a hard man, never one to let sentiment or kindness influence his business tactics." Ottilee looked down at her hands.

The car stopped, then started again with a jerk and a clang of the motorman's bell.

"Did you find out how he did it? Got the poison in your father's food, I mean. It hasn't said in the papers." Tess decided she'd better find out all the particulars while she had this chance.

"Papa always got up very early, around five," Ottilee related. "Our cook doesn't stay at our house but comes every morning at six-thirty. Jim lived over the carriage house, he took care of the horses as well as the garden; so, he would come over every morning early and serve Papa his breakfast between five-thirty and six. He would have had every opportunity to poison the food."

"It's a wonder your father trusted him, knowing how the man must feel toward him," Tess said.

"I expect Papa had forgotten about the foreclosure. It occurred almost four years ago and he foreclosed so many mortgages on houses there in East Allerton. So, when we needed a gardener last year and Jim applied for the job, I'm sure Papa wasn't aware of his motive."

Tess thought of the small houses in East Allerton, some of their occupants struggling to meet payments to buy the places. How distressing it must be when the bank took houses back and the would-be owners lost all they had paid. It was good that Grandma Barker's house was free and clear. How glad she was that she wasn't a banker, having to refuse loan extensions in the interest of the bank's depositors. Rich or poor, life had a way of being full of problems.

She left Ottilee at the "Works" and walked thoughtfully toward home. She stepped across the road to see how the greenhouse was coming along. The glass roof was across half of it and the front windows were in place in the adjoining frame building. It was a nice layout with plenty of room to expand. Now if she were running the place, she would start planting Christmas trees in that field beyond the greenhouse and some holly bushes nearby for Christmas wreaths. She had noticed how busy the stands were along the sidewalks downtown where wreaths and trees were sold in December. If she ever saw Andy out here she'd ask him about his plans.

Uncle Will was late coming in to supper. He sat on the back steps to clean the mud from his shoes, then removed them and walked into the kitchen in his sock feet.

"Sorry I'm late, Tess. Struck rock on the Simon lot. Slowed me up. Dave Simon died last night."

"Mort's son?"

"That's right. Say, Andy Herleman was over here early this afternoon. Wanted to know if I knew of a schoolboy who could help him afternoons after school and on Saturdays, when he opens the new place. Says he'll pay him a dollar and a half a week."

"Good pay for after-school work," Tess said, pouring the coffee. "Did you think of anyone?"

"Well, not when he was here. But while I was up there digging away at those blamed rocks, I got to thinking about it. And thinks I to myself, who is it thought of that greenhouse in the first place? Who is it as has got *two* green thumbs when it comes to plants and flowers? Who is it that stops over there every afternoon to see how her dream is coming along? Why, Tessie Trumper, that's who! So, I says to myself, why shouldn't Tessie have that job? She's right for it in every way. What do you say, girl?" Uncle Will eased himself into his rocker and slipped on his carpet slippers.

Tess set the coffeepot on the stove with a bang and turned toward him. "Me! But he wants a boy."

"No boy in this neighborhood who'd be the help you'd be in a place like that." Uncle Will reached for his pipe.

"But even if Andy would hire me, I'm not sure I could manage everything here along with such a job. Now don't light up, Uncle Will, supper's ready," she admonished as she sat at the table. Uncle Will put down the pipe and joined her.

"Oh, I think if I put my mind to it I could help out a little more with the housework and take over some of your chores on the hill. I was thinking that if Andy does a good business he might, in time, need a full-time person. And next spring when you graduate, why there you'd be, experienced around the place and all. This winter it'd be nice for you to have that dollar and a half coming in every week. I tell you what, you stop over there tomorrow afternoon and if Andy's around, why you just apply for the job. Say I sent you."

It wasn't until next day in school that the idea really took hold of Tess. In study hall, the picture of herself working under that glass roof, Andy teaching her to tend hothouse plants, waiting on customers, learning to make funeral wreaths and casket bouquets—well! She read the chapter on the causes of the French Revolution, but not one word took root in her mind.

After school she slammed her books in her locker and hurried to see if she could catch an earlier streetcar. If she got the job she'd have to get out there as early as possible each day. She'd just see how early she could make it.

The site of the new greenhouse seemed deserted as Tess made her way on the temporary boardwalk across the muddy ground in front. Pushing open the door of the frame building, she stepped in.

It was as though she had stepped right into her dream. There was a counter across the front, shelves on all sides, big tables in the rear upon which to work on funeral pieces, and plenty of windows for light. How many times she had seen herself behind such a counter, selling flowers, not just for funerals, but for parties and weddings. She just had to get this job!

Someone was whistling outside. She went behind the counter and out the back door. Andy Herleman looked up, his arms full of odds and ends of lumber left by the carpenters. "Why, hello there, Tessie. So you came to see my new place. It's a dandy, isn't it? I've been after Pa for a long time to let me do this. I'm trying to clean up out here. Just a minute, I'll stack this over there and I'll show you around."

"It's a beautiful setup, Andy, just beautiful," Tess said, watching him stack the lumber neatly against the building.

He led the way into the greenhouse and told of his plans for each section. He described the heating system to be installed, the latest thing, he said, with pipes that would run the length of the greenhouse on each side and down the middle. He was having a special room built onto the sales building, he went on, a room where he could stay overnight in winter. He'd have to keep the fire going all night to keep the temperature just right.

Tess drank in all this greenhouse talk, asking such pertinent questions that Andy paused beside a water faucet and looked at her intently.

"I declare, Tess, you seem as interested in this place as I am. Well, as I was saying, we had city water piped out here from Four Corners. It cost a pretty penny, but I figured we had to have it, and digging a well would have been just about as expensive." He turned on the faucet briefly to demonstrate its efficiency, then wiped his hand on a bandana handkerchief hanging from his overalls pocket. "This place has got to succeed, Tess. I got a loan from Papa and a mortgage from the bank. I make a go of it or else—!" He laughed and Tess liked the sound. "—or else Andy Herleman's goose will be cooked for sure."

"You'll make it go, all right," Tess said, looking up at the sunlit roof. "And I've come here to see if I can help you do it. Uncle Will told me you were looking for after-school help. I guess you specified a boy, but I think I can be of more help to you around here than any boy."

Andy put the bandana back in his pocket. "Well, now, I don't know, Tess. I'm going to keep a horse and wagon out here. My helper will be expected to make deliveries in town and take care of the horse too, at times. We'd be using manure as fertilizer, there'll be a lot of dirty jobs, jobs a girl's not likely to take to."

Tess laughed. "I'm not afraid of dirt or bad smells, Andy. Many a bucket of fertilizer I've carried from the Washingtons' barn to use on plants at Willow Hill. And while I've never driven a horse, I can learn. You won't find another person as interested in this greenhouse as I am. You see, I've been building one on this very spot for years, in my dreams of course," she added, then, in a more sober tone, "A mortgage is a serious thing. Any boy you might hire wouldn't realize that as I do. You need me in this establishment, Andy Herleman. If you don't hire me, you'll regret it."

Andy grinned. "You know, Tessie, I just bet I would. You've got a way of convincing a fellow. Could you begin October 1, next Saturday? I'm starting to move plants out here from our other place that day, even if things aren't finished here."

"What time should I be here?"

"Could you make it by seven?"

"Sure."

Tess ran all the way home to tell Uncle Will. He wasn't in the house. She changed her clothes and ran up the hill to find him. She paused at the willows and murmured ecstatically, "I got the job, Mama, I got the job!"

The willows rustled an answer and she ran down the other side singing,

> "Sing willow, willow, willow;
> Sing all a green willow must be my garland."

14. The Greenhouse

After supper Tess and Uncle Will planned the work at the house and on the hill so that Tess could be at the greenhouse at the specified hours. Uncle Will wrote a schedule on some brown wrapping paper and stuck it on the kitchen wall.

Rubbing his chin thoughtfully, he stood looking at it for some time. "Well, as I see it, Tess, we can do it, providing deaths and burials happen at the right times. But an epidemic in town could just blow this schedule sky-high."

Tess frowned. "Do you think I shouldn't have taken the job?"

"Course not. I've been wanting you to learn something besides cemetery business and this is a great opportunity, one cut exactly to your pattern. We'll manage."

Around four-thirty next day, Tess went to the Washingtons' to find out if Stella had heard from Irene and also to tell of the new job.

Stella stood at the stove, stirring a huge kettle of thick, vegetable soup, its appetizing aroma filling the house. "Sam stopped by there yesterday," she said in answer to Tess's question about Irene. "He said they've got a nice little place all to themselves and seemed mighty happy. Irene's getting along fine with the work. Of course, working there before, she knows how Mrs. Converse likes things done. I'll go in and see her myself when I get a chance."

Little Rachel toddled to Tess's knee and turned around to be taken on her lap. Tess lifted her up and gave her a hug, whereupon Rachel settled back contentedly and sucked her thumb.

"When do you think I should go see Irene, Stella?"

"Why don't you give her a call on your telephone? Linc or Sarah May usually answer all calls there in the kitchen, then buzz Mrs. Converse as soon as they find out who's calling."

"All right I will." Tess hesitated. "Stella, I have a job!" Enthusiastically she described her after-school employment.

Stella stirred the soup slowly. "Hmmm. Sounds good the way you tell it, honey, but I don't want to hear tell of you neglecting your school. Your mama had her heart set on you getting a high school diploma." Stella put the lid back on the soup. "You have to remember that there are only twenty-four hours in a day. You're strong like your papa and smart like your mama. You'll get along, I 'spect. But I wonder if you can manage your housework too. Let me know if things get ahead of you, and Miriam can come over and lend a hand. She's a big help. I've been depending on her more and more since Irene's gone."

"Tess you'll kill yourself!" was Donna's reaction to the new job. "All the things you do there at the cemetery and at your house, and then to add a job at a greenhouse! Well, I think you're crazy! What do you think you are? A work horse?"

Tess laughed. "No, just a Trumper and believe me they've always been strong. Papa was a blacksmith and Grandpa Trumper was a deliveryman for the Tipton flour mill. He used to heave hundred-pound sacks of flour around like they were nothing at all. Mama told me that the way he used to handle a barrel of flour was a wonder to behold," Tess said proudly.

Sunday found Tess on the streetcar. She had called Irene on Friday and the new bride had asked her to come for a Sunday-afternoon visit. Off the streetcar, Tess walked fast toward the Converse mansion. She saw Linc on the back porch hanging a broom on its hook.

"Hello, there, Linc."

"Glad to see you, Tess. Irene's up at our place waiting for you. She's mighty anxious to show you around."

"You look well and happy, Linc."

"Irene and I are very happy," he said. "She's a wonderful girl, Tess."

"Guess I know that better than anyone. How do I get up to your rooms?" Tess asked.

Linc pointed. "There's an outside stairway there the other side of the carriage house."

At the top of the stairs Irene answered Tess's knock. Tess hugged her then held her off at arm's length.

"'Renie, aren't you elegant in this stylish uniform, just like maids wear in stage plays."

Irene stepped off and turned around slowly so Tess could get the full effect of the black dress, the organdy collar and cuffs, the white apron, and the bit of lace and organdy worn across the top of her head.

"I could have changed, I have the rest of the day off, but I wanted you to see it on me. Oh, Tess, I'm so happy. Mrs. Converse is so nice to me. And Linc—well—" Irene paused.

Tess looked deep into the familiar dark eyes. "No need to say it, 'Renie. You're more in love than ever. I'm glad, glad,

glad. Now—show me the rest of your house. This is a sweet little living room. Where'd you get all the furniture?"

"From Mrs. Converse's attic."

Tess admired everything from the clothes closet with its hooks and rod to the tiny kitchen with its gas hotplate.

"Of course I don't cook much here, we usually eat with Sarah May at the big house, but Linc and I have our breakfasts here." Irene touched a small iron skillet hanging back of the hotplate, touched it lovingly, as though the fact that it held Linc's ham and eggs each morning made it especially dear to her. "Come on in the living room and sit down. Now, tell me about *you*."

"Well," Tess began as she sat down in a small Boston rocker by the living-room window, "the most important thing that's happened to me is that I've got a job!"

"A job! Oh, Tess, you haven't quit high school! If you have, Linc will be so disappointed."

"Don't fret yourself. No, I haven't quit school. But one thing is sure, I'm not wearing any such fine regalia as yours on *my* job! From now on my old work shoes and denims are my uniform." Tess described Andy Herleman's new business and the part she was to play in it. "I worked there all day yesterday," she went on, "and oh, the things I learned. Andy brought a wagonload of plants from the other greenhouse. My, but he's smart about plants, knows scientific names and all that. Remember how I took botany my sophomore year? The teacher sure didn't make it very interesting. But now I'm going to get out my old textbook and review some of the stuff. Tomorrow the workmen will start installing the heating plant. Have to get it working before the heavy frosts set in."

Irene laughed. "Tess, you almost sound like a partner in the business instead of just after-school help."

"I sort of feel like a partner. No one knows better than you how I've dreamed of a greenhouse on that spot." Tess rocked slowly. "Oh, I must tell you about Seth."

"Is he doing all right?" Irene asked.

"Just fine. He tried out for chorus on Thursday, and Friday he told me he made it. I was sure he would; any of you Washingtons could sing your way right into heaven."

"Don't exaggerate, Tessie, we're not that good. But did *you* make chorus? I remember your talk with Miss Anderson last May."

Tess stopped rocking. "I didn't try out. You see, I had just got this job on Tuesday, so I thought it foolish to try for chorus since I won't have any days free after school from now on."

Irene frowned. "I hope you haven't bitten off more than you can chew. Even *you* can't do everything." She got up and put the teakettle on to boil. She took a loaf of nut bread from a box and cut slices.

Tess stood in the kitchen doorway. "Don't worry about me, Irene. Uncle Will is going to help with the housework, he says. He's even worked out a schedule for us. Hmmm, that looks good."

"I wouldn't count on Uncle Will for much housework if I were you. He'll mean well, and start out strong, but men have a way of forgetting that housework is a day-in-day-out job, constant, never ending. They just don't have the patience for it." Irene put a napkin over the plate of nut bread. "Come back in the living room, I want to show you something." In the other room she opened a drawer in a chest and took out a tissue-paper package. "Mrs. Snyder was here yesterday and brought us this wedding present. Just look, Tess; did you ever see anything so beautiful?"

Tess stepped closer as Irene pulled aside the paper, disclosing an exquisite white linen tablecloth and six napkins. "Golly, Irene, that's just elegant. Why, I'll bet Mrs. Converse hasn't any finer than that." Tess put a forefinger under the cloth to feel the texture.

"I know she hasn't, for I've handled her linen. Mrs. Snyder is so grateful to Linc. She wanted to give him money, but Linc wouldn't take it. She made him promise though that if she could ever help him in any way he would ask her. She is a very nice lady. I'm glad it was Linc who set her free."

October flew by like a redbird through the willows, and, like the redbird, flashed its brilliant color against the sky. Each school day was only a period of time to Tess, a period to be lived through so she could be at the greenhouse.

One Saturday Donna and her father stopped in on their way to Willow Hill and Tess showed them around the greenhouse. She introduced them to Andy and, as she watched him shake hands with Mr. Grant, she felt proud that "her" greenhouse was being run by so capable a man.

She learned to hitch the horse, Jasper, to the delivery wagon and to drive into Allerton without trepidation. Late in the month she drove all the way to the north side to the other greenhouse for a load of plants. Mr. Herleman showed her that establishment; he was surprised and pleased at her interest and pertinent questions.

"Tessie, we'll make a horticulturist of you if you don't watch out. Andy tells me you take to that new greenhouse like a duck to water," he said as she drove away.

Now, that was a nice, high-sounding word, Tess thought—horticulturist, one who cultivates plants. Yes sir, that was just what she was going to be, a horticulturist. Working with Andy, she was in exactly the right place to learn to be one too. And when she learned everything, why then *she* would open a greenhouse in another part of town, she dreamed on. She'd have a little house on the premises so she could be there night and day to take care of her flowers.

But, could Allerton support three greenhouses? her practical self asked. And in another part of town she'd have to leave Willow Hill, and what would happen to Uncle Will?

She was becoming increasingly aware that, for all of his schedule on the kitchen wall and his willingness, Uncle Will was no great shakes at daily housework. As time went on she pushed out of her mind the knowledge of dust on the furniture, unironed clothes in the basket, the growing pile of undarned socks and stockings and dirty spots on the kitchen linoleum.

Fortunately, she was taking only four subjects at school and had a study period for each one, so her classwork was not suffering. But what about time to read a book for those outside-reading reports Miss Eben required? she asked herself occasionally. She didn't even have time to stop at the public library. Oh, well, the first one for seniors wasn't due until November 7. She'd look through the bookcase at home and find a book of Mama's to read.

If her housekeeping was less than perfect, Andy had no cause for complaint in her work at the greenhouse. She dug, transplanted, watered, mulched, cultivated, and pruned. She took care of Jasper and made deliveries.

Only on Sunday afternoons did she have a chance to run up to the willows, and then only briefly; so briefly in fact that she scarcely heard the whispering branches. It may have been that she didn't want to listen, fancying that their murmur was an echo of Irene's voice saying that she was biting off more than she could chew.

Saturday, October 29, was a good day, the air nippy and

invigorating. Tess whistled and sang in the greenhouse as she performed the tasks Andy had assigned. Above the glass roof was the blue sky, she had only to glance up and, there it was, a ceiling of azure and sunlight.

She had whistled through "Billy Boy," one of Uncle Will's favorites, hummed through "Juanita," a favorite of her own, and was just in the middle of the "Willow Song," singing vigorously as she swept the aisles between the plants, when Andy stepped in from the other building. Tess stopped singing and looked at him questioningly.

"Oh, don't stop," he said. "Don't know when I've had such a fine concert. I recognized 'Billy Boy' and 'Juanita,' but what was that last one?"

Tess explained.

"Shakespeare is it? Reminds me of my high school days. Our senior class put on *Julius Caesar* and I played Brutus."

"You did?" Tess's eyes brightened with interest. "I haven't read that one."

"Oh, it's a jim dandy, bloody as all get out. I can still spout my lines." He struck an exaggerated pose and began to recite in stentorian tones:

> "*The abuse of greatness is when it disjoins*
> *Remorse from power: and, to speak truth of Caesar,*
> *I have not known when his affections sway'd*
> *More than his reason. But 'tis a common proof,*
> *That lowliness is young ambition's ladder,*
> *Whereto the climber—upward turns his face;*
> *But when he once attains the upmost round,*
> *He then unto the ladder turns his back,*
> *Looks in the clouds, scorning the base degrees*
> *By which he did ascend: so Caesar may. . . ."*

Andy laughed and picked up a trowel. "I expect I could quote yards of that play. Miss Eben was a good coach and our lines had to be letter perfect. Do senior classes still put on Shakespeare?"

"Uh huh, last spring it was *Taming of the Shrew.*" Tess wished again that she had seen it. She wondered whether or not Miss Eben would accept *Julius Caesar* as a book report. She really should read it since Andy knew it so well.

Andy started toward the door. "Well, I'll leave you to go on with your singing. I suppose you belong to the high school chorus."

"No. They rehearse after school."

"Say, that's a shame." He frowned. "With a voice like yours you really should be in that group." He paused, hand on the doorknob, and looked at her thoughtfully. "Am I working you too hard, Tess?"

"Oh, no. I love every minute of it."

"Well, I don't mean to. It's just that there's so much to do. But I wish you could be in that chorus."

"Think nothing of it. I'd a lot rather be right here."

It was half-past six by the time she entered Willow Hill gate. There was a light in Uncle Will's bedroom window. Now, what was he doing up there, when he should be in the kitchen starting supper? She was as hungry as a thresher and it would take so long to peel the potatoes and cook them. Uncle Will didn't seem to realize that she had put in a hard day's work too, had been at it since seven. Farther on she could see that there was lamplight in the kitchen too.

With a sense of urgency, she ran up the back path and opened the kitchen door.

Stella looked at her from beside the stove. She held a cloth in her hand and Tess noted guiltily that she was washing off the bacon spatterings on the back of the stove, spatterings neglected for the past week. Food was sizzling in a skillet and the smell of baking biscuits tickled Tess's nose with their browning aroma.

Stella looked stern; her forehead wrinkled and her eyes narrowed as, hands on hips, she glowered at Tess.

" 'Bout time you showed up, my girl. What's been going on over here? Will stops at my house, sick as a dog. Has to come home and start supper, he says; Tessie works late on Saturday, he says. I come home with him and put him to bed. And what do I find? A house not fit for the chickens! Dust an inch thick, your bed not made, this kitchen floor like a loblolly, and scarcely enough food in the pantry to make a meal."

"Oh, is Uncle Will's cold worse?"

"So—you *did* know he had a cold, and you paid no mind to it! I declare, Tess Trumper, you are the beatingest girl! I thought you had more sense. Any outside job always has to come second to a woman. The comfort of her family must come first and Will Bagley is your family and responsibility."

Tess felt five years old. Quick tears of remorse stung her eyes. "Oh, Stella, I'm sorry. Is Uncle Will bad sick? What can I do for him? I didn't know his cold was bad. He didn't say anything."

Stella's hands dropped from her hips and she turned back to the stove. "Will wouldn't. He knows how much working at that greenhouse means to you. But Tessie," Stella's voice was less severe, "you can't let him go on like this. You are going to have to spend fewer hours over there and tend to your knitting here."

"But Andy needs me, Stella, needs me an awful lot." Tess hung her coat on the back of the door.

"Will needs you more. You talk it over with Andy. I expect he'll understand. From what Sam says, that Herleman boy's a fine young man." Stella finished cleaning the stove and hung the cloth on a rod. "Now, I've got to get along home to my own family. I've got some tansy tea brewing here on the back of the stove. You give Will a cup of that and not too much food for his supper. He ought to eat light for a couple of days." She took her shawl from the back of a chair and threw it about her shoulders, clasping it across her ample bosom. "Now to-morrow, Sunday or no Sunday, I'm sending Miriam over and I want the two of you to give this house a cleaning. Why, Agnes Trumper would turn over in her grave if she could see it. I just hope she'll forgive me for not coming over here sooner to see what was going on."

Tess followed her to the door. "Thank you, Stella." She stood a moment, then threw her arms about the woman. "You are so good to me. What would I ever do without you to set me straight!"

Stella patted her. "It's no more than I'd do for Irene or any of my others, Tessie. You belong to us too. Sorry I had to be hard on you. But young ones have to be reined in occasionally or they go so fast they forget where they're headed. I just want to keep you in the right direction. Now you take good care of Will and keep him in bed for a couple of days. Sam will be over to see what needs doing on the hill."

Tess closed the door after the departing Stella, walked slowly to the oven, took out the biscuits and put them on the back of the stove.

What should she say to Andy? Should she telephone him tonight? Would she have to give up all those hours at the greenhouse? How she would miss them. But Stella was right, Uncle Will must come first. She had been selfish and thoughtless not to have thought of his comfort. He had been so good to her and she loved him so very much.

But golly! It was going to be tough not to see Andy. She just hadn't realized until this minute how she enjoyed talking to that fellow. She didn't even think of how short he was, compared to her that is, but only thought of his broad friendly face and deep laugh. And, heavens to Betsy, how he could reel off Shakespeare! Just like a real actor!

She poured Uncle Will's tea and prepared his plate.

15. Red Carnations

Andy *was* understanding, just as Stella had predicted. Tess called his home Sunday evening and explained that she would have to spend more time at home to take care of things.

"Do you think you could continue working on Saturdays?" he asked.

"I think I can manage that. But how will you get everything done over there?" Tess thought Andy had a fine-sounding voice on the telephone. She could close her eyes and see his face.

"Well, I'll need other help on the other five days. Do you have any suggestions?"

"How about Joe Washington? He's thirteen and very dependable. He goes to Monroe Avenue school, so he could be at the greenhouse right after school. Want me to ask him?"

"I'd appreciate it if you would, Tess."

"All right. I'll go over there tonight and have him come to see you tomorrow."

"Fine." He paused. "Tess, I wonder if you'll do something for me?"

"Why—why, sure." Tess pressed the receiver closer to her ear.

"I want you to find time to get in the high school chorus. This is your last year in school, and music would be a fine experience for you."

Tess was disappointed; she had felt sure he was about to ask her to do something special at the greenhouse. She gave a short laugh. "The chorus? Oh, well—sure. If you think it important, I'll try. But it may be too late. Tryouts were some time ago."

"You explain your situation to Miss Anderson. As I remember her, she's a very nice lady."

Tess went upstairs to check on Uncle Will and to tell him she was going to the Washingtons'. He was comfortable and told her not to worry about him.

In the kitchen she put on her coat, glanced around at the spotless room, and heaved a satisfied sigh. What a good feeling to have a clean house once more! She and Miriam had given the place a thorough going over. They had both missed church this morning, but Miriam had reminded her of one of Stella's sayings, that cleanliness was next to Godliness, so her conscience was eased.

Joe was excited at the prospect of a job at the greenhouse and asked many questions about the work. The idea of caring for and driving the horse especially appealed to him.

The wind had grown brisk by the time Tess started back home; dry leaves swirled down from their branches, those already on the ground flew about like flocks of skittering sparrows. The chill against her cheek reminded her that fall's warm beauty had left Willow Hill, making way for cold, bleak winter.

At the top of the hill the willow branches were bare, their whisper now a hoarse rattle in the wind. A few more days and Willow Hill would be entirely leafless and, to all appearances, dead. It was a good thing, she thought, that she knew that it wasn't so, that life was only resting, and would spring up next April more beautiful than ever.

Last night she had been discouraged that she couldn't manage everything, couldn't spend those extra days at the greenhouse. But now she was sort of glad. It would be a good thing for Joe. He might turn out to be a horticulturist himself when he grew up. With Andy to teach him, he certainly could be if he applied himself. She felt sure that Stella and Sam would see that he did.

She had to admit that singing in the chorus appealed to her. Donna was in it. It was thoughtful of Andy to think of it. She was lucky to be working for him.

She still missed Irene, but not as much as at first. Strange the way life was; gaps were made suddenly, and then, just as suddenly were filled with new events and people helping a person to adjust and go on without loss of balance.

Tess kicked through the leaves, enjoying their crisp crackle, as she went down the hill, whistling all the way,

> *Sing willow, willow, willow;*
> *Sing all a green willow—*

At lunch period next day, Tess found Miss Anderson in the music room and explained why she hadn't tried out for chorus.

"And now that I'm not going to be working after school, why Andy thought—that is, Mr. Herleman thought—you might be willing to let me try out."

"Andy Herleman? I remember him well, has a very nice voice. Had to miss a lot of chorus rehearsals because he was on the basketball team. If I remember correctly he sang a solo at one of our spring concerts." Miss Anderson got up from her desk and walked to the piano. "All right, Teresa, what do you want to sing?"

"Andy was in chorus? Why he didn't tell me." She followed the teacher and stood beside the piano. "Do you mind if I sing the Willow Song you told me about? I looked it up in the play and I've been singing it a lot. Maybe I don't have the tune exactly right, but I've grown awfully fond of it."

Miss Anderson smiled. "Well, if you went to all the trouble to find it, sing it by all means." She struck a chord.

"That's too high." Tess leaned over and struck a lower note. "This one."

Without accompaniment, she sang the words she and Irene had learned to a tune, half right, half made up, the one with which they had annoyed Uncle Will last June.

When she finished, Miss Anderson said, "Well, the tune isn't exactly right, but the voice is good chorus material, Teresa. Think I shall put you with the altos. Rehearsal is every Thursday from three-thirty to four-thirty."

"Thank you, Miss Anderson. Andy said you were very nice and would take me."

"Oh, did he now! I must stop by his greenhouse and see him one of these days. I like to keep tab on my former pupils. I might even buy some flowers!" She laughed. "You see, Teresa, schoolteachers are people too. Compliments please them no end."

That evening Tess received a telephone call from Judge Milburn. "Today I remembered, Tess, that you have been taking care of my lot for six months. You've looked after it in fine style. Hope you'll continue to see to it and if you'll stop by I'll pay you in advance for the next six months."

"But, Judge, there really won't be anything to do in the winter. I've already pruned and covered the plants with leaves. Nothing more needs to be done till spring."

"Tess, I'd like flowers put on about once a month, even if they freeze. You work there at the greenhouse so you could easily choose something. Around Christmas I'd like a lot of nice holly and maybe a little Christmas tree for the children. Have

Andy send me the bill. You see to it, Tess. And don't forget
to stop by for your money."

She went upstairs and took her money box from a dresser
drawer. There was more than six dollars, earned at the greenhouse, and she had six dollars in the bank. If Judge Milburn
paid her twelve more, she would have twenty-four. What a lot
of money! From now on she would only be getting seventy-five
cents a week for the ten hours she worked on Saturdays; Joe
would be getting the other seventy-five cents for the ten hours
he worked, two hours a day, five days a week.

Maybe she could save enough by spring to buy a tailored
suit and a really nice graduation dress. She got up and looked
through the clothes in her closet. Ugh! Whenever she looked
at that yellow dress she got a stomach-ache, reminding her as
it did of tall Jeff Madison. Him and his handsome face! Mama
used to say, "All that glitters is not gold," and "Handsome is as
handsome does," only she said pretty. Tess had thought those
old sayings just foolishness with which grownups frightened
children into behaving in the accepted manner. But the older
she grew, the more she realized their basic truths. Experience
was a severe but thorough teacher.

Senior meetings were held twice a month in 101 to discuss
class matters. A class motto had to be chosen, a class flower,
plans made to take the class picture to hang in the front hall
with those of past graduating classes, the senior play must be
chosen to be presented in the spring, and plans made for several
class parties. Tess hadn't realized there was such a to-do about
being a senior.

During each meeting, Donna sat at a front desk busily taking
down the minutes in a tablet. Tess was sure Donna was aware
of how many times, during a meeting, the class president's eyes

were turned her way, but Donna kept her head down, seemingly intent on the notes.

It was November now and each late afternoon, walking home in the cold, Tess looked forward to the warm welcoming glow of the base-burner in the living room. Amber coals showed through the wide expanse of the isinglass doors at the front and on two sides. Little blue flames shot up through the hot coals reminding her of the blue gentians that grew among her red petunias in the side yard in summer. The base-burner was a haven of warmth in the cold house, a haven by which Tess undressed at night before making a dash for her frigid bedroom and a comfortable haven to which she ran every morning to pull on her clothes.

On Thanksgiving afternoon Tess went to the Washingtons'. Stella had told her that Irene and Linc were coming out for a while. As she watched Irene, Tess had a strange sensation, as though she were being left behind.

Irene had a new assurance and dignity. Gone was the quiet, shy girl Tess had known. Irene had bloomed, as lovely as a full-blown violet without any of the shy uncertainties of the previous bud. Safe in Linc's love and respect, working with him to achieve their goal, she had taken on Stella's air of quiet competence that Tess so admired. Irene was a woman, she herself was still a girl.

Seth was there and the family listened to his account of life at Judge Milburn's and his description of classes at high school. Tess spoke up to tell of the several measures he was to sing as a solo in a chorus number.

Joe, not to be outdone by his brother, told Irene and Linc about his work at the greenhouse. "And yesterday, Mr. Herleman told me he'd like for me to work on Saturday afternoons too."

"He did?" Tess was surprised.

"Uh huh. Said he wanted me to make deliveries, that he needed you on the place." Joe looked around at the others. "I guess Tessie knows just about everything about flowers."

"Oh, Joe, I do not," Tess denied, though she gloried in the praise. "Compared to Andy Herleman, I know nothing at all."

"Well, Mr. Herleman thinks you're doing fine anyway," Joe went on. "He told me so yesterday."

Stella glanced at Tess with pride. "Well now, isn't that fine! Sam, it looks as if our young ones are doing all right by themselves." She looked around the family circle. "I declare, things are going so well with us all, it 'most makes me afraid. Blue skies are bound to be clouded sooner or later."

Sam laughed at her. "Oh, go on, woman! Enjoy today. We sure got a lot to be thankful for." He bent over, picked up little Rachel, sat her on his foot and jiggled her up and down, causing Rachel to laugh and say, "More, more," when he stopped.

Late in the afternoon, Tess walked home thoughtfully, thinking of Irene and Linc, two fine people, so happy, so in love. Would such love ever come to her? Probably not. Who would want her? Big, too tall, ugly, a queer girl if there ever was one, more at home among the tombstones than among her peers at high school.

Thank goodness for the work at the greenhouse. At least Andy wanted her there. She must work hard, learn everything she could, and maybe, if business warranted it, he might hire her for full time after she graduated. But if he did, then there would be the problem of taking care of Uncle Will and the chores she had always done in the cemetery; come spring and summer, there would be a million things to do on the hill. Oh, well, she didn't have to worry about that right this minute. In a week it would be December and time to start thinking about Christmas. She had money of her own this year and could buy a present for each one of the Washingtons as well as Uncle Will. And she must get something very special for Irene and Linc.

She ran a way, paused at the Snyder lot to admire two large sprays of evergreens on Otto Snyder's and his mother's graves. She wondered if Mrs. Snyder and Ottilee had been out or if they had telephoned and Andy had brought these over. If he had, she wished she had been here to speak with him.

December was dry and cold. Tess appreciated not having to shovel snow, but even so, she missed the beautiful, troublesome stuff. She hoped they'd get some before Christmas. Its beauty outweighed the problems it made as far as she was concerned.

Red roses and carnations were the big sellers at the greenhouse now. Tess made a casket bouquet of red roses all by herself. Andy praised her, said he couldn't have done any better himself. Later she took Uncle Will to the new grave to point out her work. He too was impressed with her new skill.

One afternoon she stopped in town to do her Christmas shopping. Her list of names included all of the Washingtons, Uncle Will, Irene and Linc, and Donna. Before she realized it she had spent twelve dollars and thirty-five cents. Standing on the corner, her arms full of packages, she thought of another present. Maybe she'd have time to buy it before the streetcar came. She really shouldn't spend any more; if she didn't watch out, there wouldn't be enough for that suit and dress next spring. But this was important, he had been so nice to her. She hurried into Millers' Haberdashery for Men and bought a dark-blue-and-maroon-striped necktie for Andy.

On Friday, December 23, the chorus gave a special program on the stage at general assembly. Seth sang his solo bit from the front row of the group. Tess, on the back row, was proud of him, and wished Stella and Sam could have heard.

Afterward she gave Donna her present and was surprised that Donna had one for her.

"Papa and I are coming out tomorrow to get something nice for Mama. What would you suggest?" Donna asked.

Tess described the flowers, holly, and evergreen wreaths available. Donna said they would look them over.

When she got home, Tess put the things she had for Judge Milburn's lot in the wheelbarrow and pushed it up the hill. She put the holly wreath on Mrs. Milburn's grave and the small Christmas tree halfway between Baby Claude's stone and those of the other two children. She took strings of popcorn and cranberries and festooned them about the branches. She hoped the wind wouldn't blow them off. The judge would probably be here tomorrow and she wanted him to see the lot at its best.

Late Christmas Eve, Uncle Will helped her carry her packages to the Washingtons'. All the little children were in bed, "so Santa Claus could come." Only Joe and Miriam were up, assisting their parents in decorating the tree in the corner of the living room. Uncle Will and Tess helped with the ornaments, paper chains, and popcorn strings.

As they left, Stella handed Tess two tissue-paper packages. "A little something I made," she said, "and Merry Christmas to you both. Come over tomorrow if you think you can stand it. As you know, Sam and I let the young ones take over on Christmas. I 'spect we'll have a time getting them to Sunday school. Christmas on Sunday is always hard on parents, what with the little ones getting up before daylight, getting them ready for church, and a Christmas dinner to cook."

"Oh, we'll make it," Sam put in. "We always have. Good night and Merry Christmas."

The night was clear and sharp, stars shimmering brightly.

"Last year at this time we had to go around by the road because of the snow," Tess recalled as they made their way through the potter's field.

"Yes, and if we're out this time tomorrow night we'll have to go the same way, according to my bones. It's going to snow big tomorrow or my name isn't Will Bagley."

"Oh, surely not, Uncle Will! It's so clear, just look up there, not a cloud."

"Mark my words, Tessie, my rheumatic joints are the best weather forecasters in the world. It's going to snow tomorrow!"

And snow it did. When Tess wakened next morning, the ground was covered with three inches of white, and the way it was coming down, the wind whirling it in all directions, this could be a real humdinger of a blizzard, as Uncle Will had said.

They opened their gifts after breakfast, Uncle Will reminding Tess of the Christmases when she too came down before daylight to see what was in her stocking.

Uncle Will liked the shirt Tess gave him and the warm muffler Stella had crocheted. Tess thought Uncle Will had shown very good taste in selecting material for a wool dress in Alice blue, one of her favorite colors. Stella's gift to her was a green taffeta shirtwaist with a high collar that fitted snugly about her throat, giving a mature dignity that delighted Tess. She recognized the material as that of a dress Mrs. Converse had given Irene. But Stella had done such a skillful job of "making over" that no one could have guessed that it was not new material. A package Sam had delivered from Irene contained an embroidered dresser scarf and doily. Tess liked them doubly because her friend had found time to make them. She wished she were as well organized as Irene and could find time to make presents. Store-bought presents lacked character, somehow, nothing but money put into them, no touch from loving hands.

Tess had put the chicken in the oven and was starting upstairs to get ready for church when Uncle Will came in with a full coal bucket. He set it beside the base-burner, reached up and pushed aside the top opening of the stove. Tess saw him wince as he bent to pick up the bucket.

"Here, let me do that. I bet your shoulder and back are hurting again." She picked up the bucket of hard coal and emptied it into the top of the stove with a noisy rattle.

"Thanks, Tessie. Joints are giving me fits this morning."

"What do you have to do today?"

"Well, Sam and I got Moss Mummery's grave dug yesterday. I told Sam he needn't show up today. A man with children should spend Christmas Day with them. I really ought to dig the grave for the Henderson child. Funeral's not till Tuesday, but with this snow coming down like it is, the longer I put it off, the harder it'll be."

"Uncle Will, I'm not going to church. I'm going to help you. I'd rather spend Christmas on the hill with you than be any place else."

When they returned from digging little Myra Henderson's grave, they found Andy on their porch. He handed Tess a long box.

Inside, as she opened it, Andy said, "I had these ready for you last night and meant to give them to you before you left. Then I got busy with that customer and you were gone when I got back from the greenhouse." He turned to Uncle Will. "Did you see this necktie Tessie gave me, Mr. Bagley?" Uncle Will smiled and nodded as Andy opened his overcoat to show the blue and maroon stripes. "That was real cute of you, Tess, putting the package in my overcoat pocket so I didn't find it till I started home. Prettiest tie I ever had."

Tess exclaimed over the flowers in the box, a dozen long-stemmed, red carnations. By the time she had returned from the kitchen with a vase, Uncle Will had gone upstairs. Andy stood at the door and watched her arrange the flowers.

"Andy, these are the first hothouse flowers I ever had of my own." She put her nose into a carnation. "Mmm, they do smell so good! Smell like the little pinks Stella has growing by her kitchen window."

Andy smiled at her. "Yes. They belong to the pink family, Caryophyllaceae. The carnation's scientific name is *Dianthus caryophyllus*."

Tess's eyes widened. "Hold on a minute till I get pencil and paper." She rummaged in a table drawer and drew out a tablet and pencil. "Now then, I hope you can spell those big words."

Andy spelled them as she wrote.

She put down the pencil. "Dianthus," she repeated. "Pretty name, but I guess it wouldn't matter what it was called, it would be lovely belonging to a carnation."

"A carnation by any other name would be as sweet, to misquote Mr. Shakespeare," he said, buttoning his coat. "I must get along. Want to stop over at the greenhouse to check the temperature."

Tess hesitated a moment. "I—we'd be glad for you to come

back and have Christmas dinner with us. The chicken's almost done."

"Why, thank you. That's mighty nice of you. But Mom's expecting me. We've got a houseful of company—aunts, uncles, and cousins; but even so, Mom would be unhappy if I weren't there too. Merry Christmas, Tess."

"Merry Christmas, Andy. I love these carnations."

At the window she watched him go down the path to the road, then make his way through the snow to the cemetery gate.

She took her coat from the chair where she had thrown it a few minutes before, and stood with it in her arms beside the table looking down at the red carnations.

Imagine it, real cut flowers in the house at Christmas! That nice Andy! If he wasn't just about the smartest man she'd ever met! *Dianthus caryophyllus!* Imagine a person knowing that!

16. Clouds

January was a difficult month. The deep snow stayed on, new layers were added from time to time. Tess got up earlier each morning to be at Four Corners for the seven-fifteen car. The drifts across Cemetery Road slowed down even intrepid Tess Trumper. Often the streetcar was late and she walked up and down the sidewalk to keep warm. Sometimes Pete Madison arrived, opened up before the streetcar got there, and she went inside the "Works" to wait out of the wind.

There were many deaths in town, pneumonia, diphtheria, whooping cough, and measles taking their usual winter's toll. Uncle Will and Sam were at their sad business every day, a rigorous business this time of year, the frozen ground presenting strong resistance to pickax and shovel.

Tess worried about Uncle Will, he had such trouble with his joints. Sometimes in the morning she wakened when he went downstairs. She could hear him going slowly, faltering at each step. For several years he had mentioned occasionally the pain in his fingers or elbows. Now, it seemed, all of a sudden, the rheumatism had spread to every joint. Tess would hurry to get down to the kitchen to help get in the coal. But Uncle Will would say,

"No, Tessie. I must keep going. The joints loosen up when

I use them, although they hurt like sixty at first. 'Spect I'd soon be in a wheel chair if I was rich and didn't have to work. Being a working man has it advantages."

At school, end-of-semester examinations took precedence over everything. Senior meetings were canceled until February. On Saturdays, while working on funeral pieces, Tess repeated to herself history dates and quotations she was sure Miss Eben would ask for on the English examination.

One afternoon they were dismissed early for a teachers' meeting and Tess took Donna to call on Irene. Irene was polishing silver in the big Converse kitchen. Sarah May took over and told her to take the girls up to her own place.

"I'm so glad you came," she told Tess and Donna as the three sat around the small coal stove in the little living room. "I like to have company in our own house."

"Well, I don't wonder," Donna said. "This place is just darling."

"Only one thing wrong with it." Irene smiled. "It's not really ours, belongs to Mrs. Converse."

"Well, not very many people own their own places. We don't," Tess put in.

"Sure, I know. But Linc and I want a business of our own. And we are going to have one or our name isn't Johnson!" Her voice had a positive ring, her head a confident tilt. Tess marveled again at the change in Irene. Here, she thought, was an example of character development as evident as in any novel she had read. Irene Johnson had arrived!

Tess laughed. "Well, 'Renie, while you are earning money for your own business, you can do with this, I should say. Most married couples starting out in the world would give their eye teeth for such a one."

"I know, Tessie, and I am grateful, but I'm not satisfied to stay this way. Oh, I must tell you. Mrs. Snyder called on us Christmas Day, brought us a fruit cake and some holly. She wants to lend us the money to start our business, but we want to have more of a down payment first. Don't want to start with too big a debt."

Donna stopped rocking. "Such ambition, Irene! I expect you'll have to work awfully hard. Most girls would think keeping house was enough."

"I love working with Linc," Irene answered.

That was it, Tess contemplated later as she crunched along the hard-packed snow toward home; if one had a loving partner, nothing was impossible, nothing was too much work. Was that a feeling-sorry-for-herself ache in her throat because no man had appeared in her life as a possible "loving partner?" There had been Jeff; but what a dud he turned out to be. No, Tess Trumper, you must face it, you are too tall and homely for any man to ever notice you, much less love, she told herself grimly, swallowing hard to disperse the self-pity.

With the beginning of the new semester in February, life at school got back to normal. The senior class met to talk about the play. Miss Eben, who would coach the actors, sat in the back of the room listening to the discussion.

"I think we should get away from Shakespeare and do something modern," Clem White said during the discussion. "It would be a lot simpler for costumes and scenery. Now last summer the stock company did a good one called 'The Heart of Mindy McHaley.' It was just great; all about mountaineers and how this girl Mindy fell in love with a revenue man who'd come to arrest whoever was making moonshine whiskey in those parts. And here it was her father who was doing it all the time."

"A play like that won't do at all," Tess interrupted briskly. "It sounds sort of trashy to me. Since they did a comedy last year, I think we should do a tragedy and I vote for *Romeo and Juliet*. I guess it's just about the most beautiful and saddest love story there is."

"But that's Shakespeare again," Clem argued. "Now in this mountain play, there's this fellow with a black beard and he—"

"No matter what's in it, it isn't as good as *Romeo and Juliet!*" Tess exclaimed. "Shakespeare's plays apply to the present no matter what year it is." This statement seemed familiar, where had she heard it? She went on. "That's the reason we quote him so often. He's as up-do-date as day after tomorrow!"

"Bravo, Teresa," Miss Eben put in from the back of the room. "Oh, excuse me. I didn't mean to interrupt."

"Well, there seems to be a difference of opinion," the president said. "Have you got all that down, Donna?" he asked the secretary. She nodded. "I think I better appoint a play committee to meet with Miss Eben. I appoint Clem chairman and Tess cochairman, with Ottilee and Steve to serve with them."

Tess wondered afterward why she had been so vehement in promoting Shakespeare. Certainly, last spring, she too had been all for a modern play. But that was before she had read *Othello* and *Romeo and Juliet* on her own. She remembered the talk with Miss Anderson about the Willow Song in *Othello*, and she realized that she had been repeating the music teacher's ideas for the most part. Had she been showing off just because she had read a couple of plays? And then there was Andy who still remembered his part in *Julius Caesar*. Well, no matter for what reason, she was going to plug for *Romeo and Juliet*. Clem and his play about moonshiners! Ugh!

There was a spell of warm weather the week of February 13, false spring Uncle Will called it. The air grew balmy, snow began to melt, and icicles to drip. The road to Four Corners was deep with slush. Tess was grateful for the four-buckle arctic overshoes that reached above her high shoes. Uncle Will suggested that, even though it was warmer, she'd better wear her knitted-wool hood and mittens, it was likely to turn cold again at any hour.

He was right. Thursday afternoon, in history class, Tess looked out the window and watched a freezing rain set in. When school was out, the sidewalks and street were covered with a treacherous glaze of ice. Only by taking long slides could one keep one's balance. Tess set out boldly to catch her streetcar, keeping herself upright by using the ice instead of fighting it. Less-audacious girls were falling and waiting for the boys to help them up. Tess had no time for such tomfoolery. Uncle Will had two graves to dig, she hoped to get home in time to help him.

By suppertime the trees on Willow Hill were coated in ice. Tess worried about the heavy branches breaking off as the wind swept them back and forth. Ice storms had a metallic, sparkling beauty, but the danger to plants and trees deterred her full appreciation.

"It's going to be an awful day tomorrow for those two burials." Uncle Will peered out the window. "They may just have to put them off. Horses would have a time keeping their footing unless it thaws, and I have my doubts if it will."

Tess stirred the fried potatoes, set the skillet on the back of the stove, and pulled the coffeepot to the front. "I wonder if Joe was able to make deliveries today. I expect there were lots of flowers sent for Mrs. Hazleton, she was so well known."

They had just sat down to supper when there was a scuffle

on the front porch and a knock. Tess walked quickly through the dark house and opened the door.

"Who is it?" she asked in the dark.

"It's me, Joe."

"Come in, Joe, and let me shut this door. That wind is biting." The boy brushed past her and she closed the door. "Come on out in the kitchen."

Even before they reached the lighted room, Tess sensed that something was wrong. When she saw Joe's frightened face she was sure of it. "What is it, Joe?"

"It's the baby. She's awful sick. Mama says will you please phone Dr. Williams." Joe twisted his stocking cap in his hands.

Uncle Will stood up and pulled out a chair. "Sit down, Joe. Of course we'll call. Tess, Doc's number is right there on the front of the telephone book. You ring him up." Tess went to the telephone. Uncle Will turned to Joe. "What seems to be the trouble with little Rachel? I didn't think there was anything Stella couldn't cure."

"It's—it's her throat. It's so sore and she's having trouble breathing. When I got home from the greenhouse, I found Papa and Mama working over her. I came here as fast as I could over the short cut. It's slow though, all that ice on top of the snow."

Tess had the doctor's house by this time and his wife was calling him from his supper.

"Dr. Williams, this is Tess Trumper at Willow Hill. The Washingtons' baby is very sick, little Rachel. Could you come out this evening and have a look at her?" There was a pause. "Yes, I know the streets and roads are mighty slick . . . Joe says it's a bad sore throat and she's having trouble breathing . . . It takes about half an hour, I'd say . . . Sure, I can take you the short cut . . . All right, I'll watch for you. I think there's a car leaves the streetcar station at six-thirty. Maybe you can make that one . . . All right, Doctor, I'll send word you're coming. . . ." Tess hung up the receiver. "He's taking the streetcar, says his horse had such a time on the icy streets this afternoon. Now Joe, you tell your folks. I'll bring him just as soon as he gets here. He said he knows Stella wouldn't send for him if it weren't serious and he'll make it as quickly as he can. You tell her that, Joe."

"Thanks, Tessie." He put on his cap.

"Why don't you sit down and have some supper before you go back," Uncle Will suggested.

"Thanks, Uncle Will, but I couldn't swallow anything. I'll get along home. Maybe I can do something."

When he was gone, Tess looked at the clock, figuring how long it would be before Dr. Williams arrived. She and Uncle Will tried to eat but had little appetite. Tess was seeing plump little Rachel toddling around the Washingtons' kitchen, seeing her back up to be taken on a lap, her eyes big as she settled back and sucked her thumb. Tess remembered the baby's glee at being jiggled on Sam's foot Thanksgiving Day. Tess swallowed hard, recalling the velvet softness of the child's skin and the dimples in her plump elbows.

They gave up trying to eat; Uncle Will sat in his rocker and Tess hurried through the dishwashing. By seven she had on her arctic overshoes, heavy coat and hood, and was at the window watching for the doctor, although she knew he couldn't possibly be coming through the gate until seven-twenty, the road from Four Corners being as slick as it was.

Finally she said, "I'm going out to the gate and wait for him, Uncle Will. I've got to be doing something."

"All right. Do you think I should call Irene and Linc?"

"Why don't you wait till Dr. Williams sees her. It may just be croup." Tess opened the door.

"I doubt if it's croup. Stella knows how to handle that, she's had enough experience with it, goodness knows. When'll you be back?"

"I'll stay as long as I'm needed."

Tess slid down the path to the road in front of the house, then walked along the side, out of the slippery ruts; her feet crunched down through the icy crust at every step. At the cemetery gate she stopped and looked down the road toward Four Corners. There was no one in sight. A light gleamed from the room back of the greenhouse. Andy stayed there nights now, to keep fires up so temperatures would be right in the greenhouse.

The freezing rain had stopped, leaving trees, bushes, telephone wires, and the snowy ground a complete glaze of shimmering ice. The sky had cleared and stars were out. The cold wind made Tess pull her coat collar up in the back and she tucked her mittened hands in her sleeves for extra warmth. She closed her eyes and prayed for little Rachel, and that the doctor would come soon.

The fifteen-minute wait seemed an hour. The sight of a figure approaching, carrying the familiar black bag, brought relief to the tension in her throat. Dr. Williams had cured her many times when Stella's remedies had failed, now he would surely cure Baby Rachel.

The doctor followed her through the gate, past the house, and on up the hill. She repeated to him what Joe had said.

"Do the Washington children go to Monroe Avenue school?" he asked.

"Yes."

The doctor gave a faint, "Hmmm."

The crunch of their footsteps blended with the crackle of the ice-coated willow branches clanging in the wind at the top of the hill.

"This is quite a sight from up here," Dr. Williams said. "I've never been out here at night. And will you look at those tombstones! Ice all over them! Real pretty, I'd say, in a cold, ghostly way. You like it out here, don't you, Tess?"

"Oh, yes. Wouldn't want to live anywhere else. Right over there is your lot, Doctor." She pointed.

"Well, so it is. I haven't been out here for quite a spell. Mother and Father are there."

"And your brother, Edward, and sister, Margaret," Tess said as they started down the hill.

"It's uncanny, Tess, the way you know these folks out here."

"Oh, I don't know, Doctor, you know the streets in town where your patients live; I know the lots where these people lie. Playing here as a child and helping tend the grounds as I've grown up, it's just natural."

"You're an amazing girl, Tess. Your folks would be proud of you. What're you going to do when you get out of high school?"

"I'd like to work full time at the greenhouse. I've been working there on Saturdays all winter. But Uncle Will's rheumatism is bad sometimes and he often needs me here."

"Yes, I heard Andy Herleman had opened up a new place out here. How's he doing?"

"Very well, it seems to me."

"A fine boy, Andy. I brought him into the world, and I've been proud of the job ever since. How much farther now?"

"Just around the bend in the river. These tracks here are

Joe's." They plodded on farther. "Now, there, you can see the lights in the house."

The doctor removed his high arctics, overcoat, and muffler in the Washingtons' kitchen, Sam watching anxiously. The children stood around looking on, awed by the fear in their father's eyes.

Tess hung her own coat on the back of the pantry door. "Is Stella with her?" she asked Sam.

"Yes, she's in there." He nodded toward his and Stella's bedroom off the kitchen.

"Tess," Dr. Williams said, "I wonder if you'll take the children in the living room. I'll want to have a look at all of them after I see Rachel."

Joe got a lamp from the corner cupboard, lit it, and led the way to the front of the house. Tess took small John's hand and gave it a reassuring squeeze as they followed.

In the living room, Joe poked the fire in the stove, put in more wood and two big lumps of coal from the bucket nearby. Tess sat in a rocker and held Johnny on her lap. A few gentle rockings and he was asleep. Danny leaned against Miriam on the couch and closed his eyes. "Shouldn't we put them to bed, Tess?" Joe asked.

"We'll wait awhile, Joe, for Dr. Williams to come in and look at them. He may think Rachel has something contagious."

"What's the matter with Rachel?" Ruth asked. "Is she going to die and be put in a little box like Cousin Marie?"

"Hush, Ruthie," Miriam admonished. "Of course not. Dr. Williams is here."

The little clock on the organ ticked loudly. The wide-eyed fear in the faces of the children dismayed Tess. She hugged Johnny close and began singing a song she had learned in first grade.

"Baby dear, baby dear, don't you cry.
Mother will come to you by and by.
Father is tending the hay and wheat,
Mother is baking a cake to eat."

She sang the many verses. The children relaxed. Nat got off his chair and sprawled on the rug beside the stove. Miriam put the sleeping Danny's head in her lap and lifted his feet on the couch. Tess sang on; all the Mother Goose songs her mother had taught her, the Willow Song and those she had learned in chorus.

At last Dr. Williams came in. Tess looked at him questioningly. The slight shake of his head kept her silent. At the doctor's bidding, each child opened his mouth to have his throat examined, Joe holding the lamp near.

"Now, I'm going to give each of you a shot of antitoxin so you won't get Rachel's sickness. Roll up your sleeves. You too, Tess."

The injections over, the doctor turned to Tess. "Get them to bed now."

"Joe and Miriam can do that. Want me to take you back?" Tess set sleepy Johnny on his feet.

"No. I'm staying until there's a change in the baby."

"Diphtheria?" Tess whispered the dread disease that the word antitoxin had suggested.

The doctor nodded and left the room.

Tess followed him to the kitchen and made a pot of strong coffee. Nine o'clock wore on to ten. Dr. Williams came out of the bedroom, drank a cup of the black liquid, and took two cups in to Sam and Stella who refused to leave the bedside.

There were several cases of diphtheria in the Monroe Avenue

school, Dr. Williams told Tess. The children had probably brought it home to Rachel.

Sitting in Stella's kitchen rocker, Tess thought about this doctor. He had had office hours today, had made innumerable house calls, and now was spending the night trying to save the Washingtons' baby. Gentile or Jew, Protestant or Catholic, black or white, rich or poor, all were one to Matthew Williams, M.D. He would fight as hard to heal Rachel Washington as he had to save Otto Snyder.

Tess dozed a little in her chair and roused when the doctor came out for another cup of coffee at eleven-twenty.

Little Rachel Washington breathed her last at two-fourteen in the morning. Tess went into the bedroom at the doctor's request and led Stella into the kitchen. Covering her face with her hands, the mother moaned softly as she sat in the rocking chair.

Tess insisted that she drink some coffee. Sam talked with the doctor about arrangements.

"Don't think about that, Sam," Tess said. "I'll call John Bixby as soon as it's daylight. He'll come out and take care of things. You want her buried on that lot on your own land where your parents and grandmother are buried?" Sam nodded. "All right. Uncle Will and I'll take care of it, you just stay with Stella and the children, they'll need you. I'll call Irene as soon as I think the Converses will be up. If I call that grocery on the corner there, would they give Grandma Barker the message?" Sam nodded again.

"You go along home, Tessie," Dr. Williams said. "There are no streetcars back to town till six-thirty, so I'll stay here and try to get a cat nap on the couch. You get some sleep. These folks will need you tomorrow."

Tess put on her wraps, then knelt beside Stella. "I'll be back in the morning, Stella, just as soon as I attend to everything. I know Irene, Grandma, and Aunt Susan will come as soon as they can."

"Thank you, Tessie. Please call the Milburns and tell Seth. I need my big boy, Tessie, I need him. He's strong, that boy, so strong." Stella leaned her head against the chair back and closed her eyes.

Tess got up, bent down and kissed the sorrowing face. "You're strong too, Stella. You've been strong for all of us."

"My strength's all gone now, Tessie, all gone."

"There's strength in the Lord, Stella. You told me that when Mama died. Now it's time for you to lean on His strength."

"I'm leaning, Tessie, I'm leaning."

Outside, the cold, brisk wind swept the weariness from Tess. With the moon reflecting a blue iridescent light from the ice-glazed snow, the world was tinsel and silver. Tess glanced toward the Washingtons' family burying ground near the potter's field. She and Uncle Will would dig the grave, she thought, Sam must not do it.

When she called John Bixby in the morning, she would tell him to use the little white hearse and she would pay for the extra charge. Stella would like it. What was the use of having money if you didn't use it for your friends?

She must call Andy too in the morning and say she and Joe wouldn't be at work.

At the top of the hill she thought of Irene. Irene could help Stella more than anyone else right now, Irene was so mature these days. If only she herself could feel mature and efficient; if she could have said something more comforting to Stella.

The ice-coated branches above the A B C stone creaked and

groaned in the wind. Tess gave a short sob. "Oh, Mama, take care of little Rachel out there. She's so little and alone."

Plodding down the hill through the crust-topped snow, Tess saw sparkling, moonlit Willow Hill through a steady flow of tears.

17. Gravedigger

She slipped into the house without waking Uncle Will, took off her clothes and dropped into bed, resolving just to close her eyes and rest, sure that she couldn't sleep with so much on her mind, so many details to attend to, come morning.

When she opened her eyes, she blinked at the brilliant sunlight. Uncle Will stood in the doorway. She sat up, reality returning with a sharp stab.

"Oh, Uncle Will, what time is it?"

"Seven. I waited up until twelve. How is Rachel?"

Tess pushed back the covers and put her feet on the cold floor. "She's gone, Uncle Will. Died about two. Diphtheria."

"Oh, my, my!" Uncle Will clicked his tongue. "Such a sweet little lamb! What can we do?"

Tess explained about the telephone calls to be made. Uncle Will said he would start breakfast while she dressed.

Tess was glad that Linc answered the phone when she called the Converse home. He would break the news to Irene gently. The grocer in East Allerton readily consented to send his boy to the Barkers' with the message and John Bixby said he would be right out to take care of things at the Washingtons'. Tess explained about wanting him to use the white hearse on the day of the funeral and that the bill was to be sent to her.

She called Andy last. He was extremely sympathetic. "Tess,

I want to do something for that family. During the time Joe has worked for me I've come to know about all of them. They are fine people. What do they need?"

"Nothing special that I can think of, just the love of their friends and relatives."

"I'll send some flowers, of course, but if you think of any way at all that I can be of service, call me. Promise?"

"I promise, Andy."

She stood at the telephone a moment. Andy had such a nice voice on the phone, so deep and masculine. She would miss working with him today.

"I'll wait until after those two burials this afternoon before I get at Rachel's grave," Uncle Will said. "Good thing the sun's melting the ice. The roads will be sloppy but not as slippery as yesterday."

"I'll help you. Sam told me the exact spot where they want to bury her. As soon as I call Mrs. Brubaker, I'm going to roast the chicken I got for our Sunday dinner and take it over to Stella. I expect the Barkers will bring food too when they come out."

Tess worked in the kitchen all morning preparing food to take to the Washingtons. Mrs. Brubaker had said she would bake a ham and some pies for the bereaved family.

At one o'clock Tess climbed the hill, a heavy market basket on her arm. At the Washingtons' she found things in the capable hands of Aunt Susan. Irene had persuaded her mother to go to bed. Irene, herself, was sewing on a pale-pink silk dress for Baby Rachel.

"I stopped and bought the material before I came," she explained to Tess. "I know how Mama favors pink, just as you do. Mr. Bixby told us about the white hearse you ordered, Tess.

Such a nice thing for you to do. Mama has always admired it, but didn't think we could have it."

"I'd like to know why not. Sweet little Rachel will be the dearest baby in heaven and she'll look like an angel in that pink dress. When is the funeral?"

"Tomorrow afternoon at our church there in East Allerton. Mama was going to have it here at home until she heard about you providing the white hearse, then she wanted it at the church so Rachel could have a long ride in it. Being on Sunday everybody can come." Irene wiped her eyes in order to thread her needle. "I don't believe any Negro child has ever ridden in that hearse. It's sort of a symbol to Mama and Papa, like Seth going to high school."

"And like Joe working for Andy Herleman," Tess added. "He's learning a lot at the greenhouse. Andy is a wonderful teacher."

Irene looked across at Tess thoughtfully. "Yes, I know."

On her way home, Tess stopped at the Washingtons' family burying ground and stuck a stick in the snow where Rachel's grave was to be dug. She'd go home and change her clothes. Uncle Will had probably finished with the burials and they would come back here and get at this job.

At home, Uncle Will was not in his rocking chair by the kitchen window as she expected. She called out and heard a response from upstairs. She found him lying on his bed with his shoes off.

"What's the matter, are you sick, Uncle Will?"

"Tessie, can you beat it? I managed to get through all the slipperiness on Willow Hill today, then I'll be dad-burned if I didn't slip in the kitchen on some water I spilled from the tin cup when I got a drink of water. Got kind of a bad sprain in the left ankle there. Feels like it's swelling up. Is it?"

Tess took off his sock and was dismayed at the enlarged ankle. "I'm going to bandage it right away," she said decisively. "I saw Stella do it once for Seth when he fell out of the hay mow."

She tore strips from an old sheet and bound the ankle. "Now you're not to stand on it," she ordered with Stella-like authority.

"But, Tessie, I've got to get at Rachel's grave."

"Now, never you mind. I'll attend to that."

"Tessie, you can't do it by yourself. The first four or five inches of ground is like a rock this time of year."

"I can do it, Uncle Will. It will be a small one. You must stay in bed."

"Well, I'll stay put here, but you go over and get Sam to help you. You can't do it alone."

In her room, Tess fastened her work skirt high at the belt so that it reached only a few inches below her knees. She didn't want a long, worrisome skirt in her way.

At four o'clock a strange figure ascended the hill. With Uncle Will's fur cap on her head, the ear flaps pulled down, his big work gloves on her hands, her sweater bulging with the extra jacket worn under it, and her short skirt flapping in the wind above her high arctics, Tess would have laughed at her ludicrous appearance if the task before her had not been so sad and difficult. She carried the pickax, shovel, and yardstick over her shoulder.

She would not go for Sam. He must not be called upon for this. Of course if she went over there someone else would probably come and help her. But she wanted to do this all by herself, for Stella and Sam, they had given her so much.

She had thought once of calling up Andy and asking him to help her. But without either herself or Joe at the greenhouse, he had his hands full today, she was sure.

First she cleared off the snow, then measured the spot as she often had done for Uncle Will. Working with pickax and shovel, she found that the ground was just as hard as Uncle Will had said. Soon, in spite of the cold wind and the disappearing warmth of the sun, Tess was perspiring. She discarded the sweater and pushed up the ear flaps of Uncle Will's cap. She swung the pickax, she dug with the shovel, gritting her teeth hard at each intense exertion. Once, when the grave was near completion, she paused and leaned against the side. To think of darling little Rachel down here in this darkness was too awful. She choked back her sobs. How did Uncle Will and Sam do this depressing work day after day? Of course they weren't usually digging graves for close friends or relatives. It was easier to be objective about death and burial when it was someone you didn't know.

She swallowed hard and went back to the task. If she didn't keep at this it would be dark before she was through, the light was fading so fast. She stuck her shovel in, pushed it down with her foot, and heaved the dirt up over the side of the grave onto the pile at the top.

"Tess, is that you?"

She looked up into Andy's astonished eyes. "Oh, hello. I didn't hear you. I'm just about finished here." She dug up another shovelful of dirt.

"Tess, why are you doing this?" Tess explained about Uncle Will's ankle.

"Well, I'm provoked," Andy went on, "I told you to call me if there was anything I could do. Did you think I didn't mean it? Here, give me your hand and I'll help you out, I'll do the rest."

"No," Tess said stubbornly. "I'll finish this myself. Want to do it for Rachel," she mumbled as she continued to toss up the dirt.

Andy watched her silently. When the grave was finished she put her hands up for his assistance. Putting down a large package, he helped her out. He picked up her shovel and pickax.

"I'm on my way to the Washingtons'," he said. "I made a small casket bouquet of pink carnations. Do you think that will be right for the child?"

"Just right. Stella loves pink and Irene made a pink dress for Rachel. Here, I'll take those." He handed her the implements. "I had to get this done today. The funeral is tomorrow afternoon at the Bethel Baptist Church."

"Well, then, I'll bring our carriage out to take some of the family. I'll ask what other transportation they'll need and see what I can do about it."

"Oh, Andy, that's good. You're very kind and thoughtful."

He picked up the package of flowers and then stood very still, looking at her. "Did you know, Tessie, that you are quite a girl? Stubborn as a mule," he smiled, "but what a girl!"

He was standing on a rise of ground and she had to look up into his face. It was nearly dusk, but his features were clear to her, for what she couldn't see, her memory filled in. She hadn't realized that she knew his face so well. For a moment she forgot the sad task she had just performed, forgot Stella and Irene. There was only Andy and herself here in the dusk of a cold winter night.

The wind blew sharply, its blast bringing her back to earth. She put down the digging tools and put on her sweater. "Well, Andy Herleman, if I'd known that digging a grave would impress you so much, I'd have dug one long ago."

"I've been impressed by you for some time," he said.

When she got home and saw the state of her clothes she wondered how he could have looked at her at all, much less have been impressed. She was clay mud, from Uncle Will's cap down to the soles of her arctics.

The Bethel Baptist Church was full the next afternoon. There had been quite a procession of carriages and buggies following the little white hearse through the streets of Allerton. Judge Milburn drove his carriage, Andy his, Linc drove one loaned by Mrs. Converse, and Mrs. Snyder provided three, her own and two she hired from the livery stable.

Tess and Uncle Will sat with the Washingtons; Stella said they seemed as much like family as the Barkers. The judge was there and his housekeeper, Mrs. Crawford. Seth had really made a place for himself in that household, Tess thought. Looking about, she spotted other white faces among the darker ones; Mrs. Snyder and Ottilee, and many from East Allerton, friends of the Barkers. Death and sorrow made all as one.

The choir sang, their voices rolling out with plaintive sadness. The people wept; the small carnation-covered casket at the front seemed so alone and pitiful.

Reverend Harrison spoke, his deep, rich voice giving words of comfort to the family. Tess thought she had never heard so warm, so meaningful a funeral message. The minister's vivid words gave such a real picture that she could see little Rachel, right this minute, walking in Heaven, trustingly holding the hand of Jesus, her little pink dress fluttering in a gentle breeze as the two of them walked the golden streets.

Tess glanced at Stella, her tear-stained face transformed as she too saw her little one being taken "home." She murmured softly, "Amen, Lord, Amen."

Tess went to school next morning in a daze. The weekend had seemed another world, so much had happened. She had difficulty giving attention in class, and during study periods her mind continued to wander. Among the scenes and events of the last two days, one kept returning: Andy, there beside Rachel's grave, saying, "Stubborn as a mule, but what a girl!" It wasn't so much what he said as how he had said it. Maybe she would stop at the greenhouse on her way home and tell him how pretty she thought Rachel's casket bouquet.

As she got off the car at Four Corners, Joe drove by. Seeing her he pulled up.

"Want a lift, Tess?"

"Sure. Been delivering in town?" she asked as she climbed to the wagon seat beside him.

"Yeah, over on Jackson, not far from here."

"How's your mother today?"

"Pretty good. She cries some, but you know Mama, she can handle trouble."

"I do indeed. Knows how to help others handle it too." Tess put her feet on the low dashboard. "It was a lovely funeral."

"Wasn't it, though? Papa and Mama were so proud having that little hearse and a casket bouquet made out of such beautiful carnations. Shall I drive you on down to Willow Hill gate? I'm sure Mr. Herleman wouldn't mind."

"No, just drive in at the greenhouse, I want to speak to Andy."

She found him in the sales room, sitting at the desk. He looked up as she opened the door.

"Well, well, good afternoon, Tessie. How's school?" He stood back of his chair.

"Oh, all right, I guess. I wasn't much good today. Kept thinking about the weekend. You know how it is. I wanted to tell you how lovely that casket bouquet was you made for Rachel. Stella and Sam were so pleased. Irene told me that Stella took three of the carnations off at the last to press in their big Bible."

"I heard about you providing John Bixby's little hearse and the white ponies. Nice thing for you to do. Didn't you tell me you were saving your money for graduation clothes?"

"Well, yes, but somehow they don't seem important now. The senior girls decided they would wear light-colored graduation dresses or white, either one. Thought a mixture would be pretty. Think I'll just wear my Sunday white one."

"How about that one you wore last Fourth of July, the yellow one? I remember seeing you on the streetcar and thinking it mighty pretty."

"The yellow one? Oh, that—well, you see—" She stopped. She couldn't explain why she didn't like that dress, the dress that, in spite of all her efforts at removing them, still had faint shadows of grass stain on the back. She changed the subject. "Our play committee met this morning and decided on *Romeo and Juliet*," she informed him.

"So you talked that fellow out of his idea about the moonshine play." Andy laughed.

"No, just outvoted him. I think he wanted to play the villain with the beard."

"What part are you going to try out for?"

"Me? Oh, I'd be no good in a play. I'm too tall. I'll help with costumes, scenery, or properties, I suppose. Miss Eben always has jobs for all the seniors when it comes to the play."

"Tessie, you are *not* too tall for anything. That's one of the many things I admire about you, your height and the fine way you carry yourself." He sighed. "Growing up, I wanted to be tall, stretched myself up like the very dickens to take advantage of every inch, but now I've become resigned to being a little man, learned to forget it for the most part." He picked up his pencil and put it in his shirt pocket.

Tess looked at him thoughtfully. "You know, Andy, I read a book once about a short man, it said he was short of stature but he cast a great shadow and everybody in town loved him."

"What book was that, Tess? I'd better read it and get some pointers."

"The Little Minister."

"Oh, but I'm no minister, just a struggling florist. But say, we've gotten off the subject—your play. You must try out for a part. I want to come and see it and I'll expect to see you up there spouting Shakespeare to a fare-thee-well."

"One thing sure," Tess replied with a grin, "I'm not the Juliet type. I'm so big, the balcony would give way. Romeo wouldn't have to climb up, I'd fall right at his feet." She laughed, then added soberly, "But Andy, I'm no actress at all."

"You never can tell till you try. Who knows, you may be as good an actress as you are a gravedigger. And that, Tess Trumper, would make you *some* actress!"

Walking home, Tess thought about it. Should she try for a part and could she get one if she tried? There was Lady Montague and Lady Capulet, two pretty good parts as she remembered; but other than Juliet, the best parts were men's. But there *was* Juliet's nurse; she was important too, and had some comedy in a few scenes. Being tall wouldn't matter in that part, in fact it might help; it would make Juliet seem all the more fragile and appealing in contrast. She wished she had the book at home, she'd like to read the play again with the nurse in mind.

How good it would be if she had Irene around to talk with about all this. Irene would tell her if she could do it or not. Irene knew her better than she knew herself. But Irene had a new life, one that did not include her except on the fringes. When a girl married she lived her husband's life. If she didn't, the marriage was wrong. Tess wondered, if she ever married, if she could be that selfless. How could she bear to leave Uncle Will and Willow Hill? She laughed at herself. This was something that need not worry her at all—marriage.

She hoped Uncle Will had stayed off his ankle today. Sam would have taken care of things on the hill. When she got home she would look in the bookcase for Mama's copy of *The Little Minister* and take it to Andy tomorrow. Reading it would show him what good things a small man could do. It might encourage him too in the thought that someday he might find a wife as tiny and as charming as the little minister's Babbie.

What was that he had said? "You may be as good an actress as you are a gravedigger. And that, Tess Trumper, would make you *some* actress!"

She stuffed her hands in her pockets, gave a little run, and took a slide on a smooth piece of ice in the road. Andy Herleman had a way of making her feel good and—and—important!

18. The Play's the Thing

The senior class decided upon April 13 and 14 as the dates for their play. Copies of the high school edition of *Romeo and Juliet* were ordered and tryouts were to take place as soon as the books arrived.

When Tess went to work the following Saturday she was surprised to see, on Andy's desk, a library book, *Shakespeare's Tragedies*. She was leafing through it as he came in from the greenhouse.

"So—here's the reason I couldn't find this book at the library yesterday," she said. "You had it."

"That's right. I finished *Romeo and Juliet* last night. Had to see what kind of thing your class is going to do."

"What did you think of it?"

"Well, of course it's not in it with *Julius Caesar*." He grinned. "But I think it will do for the class of 1911. Did you decide which part to try for?"

Tess flipped through the pages. "I thought maybe I could do the nurse. What do you think?"

Andy pursed his lips and nodded. "Lots of possibilities in that part, some very good comedy." He paused. "You know, as I read that play, I got to thinking what a lot of dudes those rich young fellows were, they had much too good opinions of themselves. They were really just a lot of show-offs, even Romeo."

"Oh, but Andy, he was so romantic and some of his lines are just wonderful. That part about wishing he was a glove on Juliet's hand so he could touch her cheek." Tess gave a long sigh as she closed the book. "What do you want me to do this morning?"

Andy laughed. "Juliet, do you think you could come down to earth long enough to pot those begonias?"

"That I could, Romeo, that I could, indeed!"

She hummed as she entered the greenhouse. Hands in dirt, she remembered that she had intended to ask him if he had finished *The Little Minister*. Imagine him making a special trip to the library to get that play! It was nice to have someone take a special interest in her doings. Uncle Will had no feel for Shakespeare, nor had Stella, and Irene wasn't around any more for discussions. How Mama would have liked the idea of her being in a play. Mama must be glad that Andy was encouraging her.

All day she worked with light heart, remembering only occasionally the tragedy of last week; it was as though it had happened months before. Noting her tendency to forget the sorrow, she wondered if it were because she was young and life was so full that she felt happy in spite of a death that had touched her so deeply. At any rate, she hummed and sang in the greenhouse and once whistled a few bars of the Willow Song.

About half-past four Joe came in from the barn after making deliveries. Tess was washing her hands at the back of the sales room. Andy looked up from his desk.

"You're back early, Joe. You had no trouble finding the place on Marion Avenue?"

"No, sir. The houses didn't have numbers on them, but I just looked till I saw one with a crepe on the door. And that was it."

"Good. Now, Joe, you just sit yourself down right here at my desk. Tess and I are going to put on a performance for you." Andy rose, picked up the library book, and opened it at a marked page. "Come on, Tess, let's read some of this so you can begin to get the feel of the nurse's lines. Don't want you to go to the tryouts cold. Here in Act Two, Scene Five, I'll read Juliet's lines and you do the nurse."

Tess finished drying her hands and joined Andy in front of the desk, thinking all the while what a surprising man he was. What other employer would take the time to help an employee get a part in a play?

She stood beside him, holding one side of the book. He pointed. "I'll start here." Then, in a high voice, he read Juliet's lines.

"O honey nurse, what news?
Hast thou met with him? Send thy man away."

Before Tess could read the nurse's part, Joe burst out laughing, saying, "Oh, Mr. Andy, you sound so funny."

Andy looked at him in feigned sternness. "Control thyself, Audience, or thou wilt find thyself tossed out upon thine ear. We'll brook no levity here." Joe clapped his hand over his mouth, his eyes still merry. Andy went on. "In Shakespeare's time women's parts were *always* taken by men, mostly boys no older than yourself. Now, Nursey!" He turned to Tess. "Read thy lines."

Stifling a giggle, Tess began. Andy stopped her.

"No, no, Tess. You are an elderly, plump lady who has been rushing around on your mistress' errand. You are out of breath, so out of breath that you can't give the news. She says her bones ache. Maybe she had rheumatism, so she would walk as though her joints were stiff. You must practice that. Now read, and all out of breath, remember." He gave her the cue.

Tess read breathlessly:

"I am weary, give me leave awhile.
Fie how my bones ache, what a jaunce have I had!"

"That's better," Andy encouraged. "I think she might, at this point, fan herself with her hands. I've seen my mother do that when she has been hurrying about."

After a while Joe lost his inclination to laugh at Andy's high, Juliet voice, and listened quietly as Andy interspersed the reading with explanations of the nurse's character.

"She's old, Tess. She's taken care of this fourteen-year-old Juliet since the girl was a baby, so she will speak to her as though she were scolding. Now, read that speech."

Tess read in a cracked voice,

"Lord how my head aches, what a head have I!
It beats as it would fall in twenty pieces.
My back a tother side, oh my back, my back!
Beshrew your heart for sending me about
To catch my death with jauncing up and down."

"Now you're getting it. That voice is just right. Oh, I tell you, Tess, this is a wonderful part. You'll have the time of your life doing it. The audience will love you."

"Not so fast, Andy." Tess laughed. "I haven't got it yet."

"You will, because no other senior is going to understand this nurse as you do." Andy pulled up the bench from the wall where customers often sat while waiting for orders to be filled. "Let's sit down while we do the rest of this scene." He looked across at Joe. "If you're tired listening to all this Joe, you can run along home."

"I'd like to listen, Mr. Andy, if it's all the same to you. Mama's always telling me to keep my ears open and learn something. I reckon this is one of those times."

Andy laughed and looked back at the book. "All right, Joe, keep your ears alert and learn some Shakespeare."

At ten minutes to six, Andy closed the book. "Well, Miss Trumper, if you read for Miss Eben like that, I'd say the part is yours."

"If I get it, it will be because of your coaching. How'd you manage to get the feel of this play so well after reading it just once?"

"Well, as I remember, we talked about it some when I was in school and I had read the story in Lamb's *Tales from Shakespeare*. And I guess, maybe, in a former incarnation, I must have been an Elizabethan." Andy rose and put the book on the desk, laughed, and winked at Joe. "Otherwise how would you account for my magnificent performance in the role of Brutus, there on the stage of dear old Allerton high. Who knows, the Bard himself may have coached me in my former life."

"Oh, Andy, I haven't watered those new shoots, yet," Tess said as she moved the bench back into place.

"Don't bother. I'll do it. I'm staying here tonight. I think we're in for another cold snap. Did you bring in enough coal for tonight, Joe?"

"Yes, sir."

"All right, you get along home. Oh, Tess, here, I want to return your book. Thanks very much for letting me read it. That Gavin Dishart was a great little fellow. Sort of a good example for all of us short guys to follow. Was it you who marked certain passages in it?"

Tess took *The Little Minister*. "No. It was Mama's book, she did the underscoring. She loved the story."

"Your mother must have been a very wonderful, sensitive woman."

"She was, Andy, she certainly was."

Joe walked home with her. When they reached the porch, he peered up into her face in the darkness.

"You've been mighty still tonight, Tessie. Anything wrong? Did I make you mad, laughing the way I did; but Mr. Andy did sound funny pretending he was a woman."

"Oh, no, Joe. I'm not mad at you, not at all. In fact, right this minute I just love the whole world!"

Joe made his way up the hill wondering what had gotten into Tessie.

Tess went inside, vowing to look in *The Little Minister* at the first opportunity to see what passages Mama had underscored.

The play books arrived on March 2. Miss Eben gave them to those who wanted to try out, so they could read the play overnight. After school next day she met with the class and said,

"Now we have thirty-five in the class, so of course there will not be speaking parts for everyone. In this shortened version of the play some of the male roles are eliminated. But everyone can appear on the stage at some time or another in the crowd scenes. Over the years we have collected a very fine wardrobe of Shakespearean costumes. Everyone can appear in suitable clothes."

Donna nudged Tess and whispered, "So that's the reason we always do Shakespeare; got to air the costumes once a year to keep out the moths."

Tess suppressed a giggle.

Miss Eben went on. "We have fourteen girls in the class and there are only four speaking parts for women, so most of you will appear but will have no lines. Now how many would like to read for Juliet?"

All the girls except Tess held up their hands. Miss Eben smiled. "Well, Teresa, you seem to be the only one who doesn't think she wants to play a fourteen-year-old."

"No, ma'am. I'm sure I'm not the Juliet type," Tess said. The others laughed. Tess was glad Andy had helped her identify herself so strongly with the nurse, otherwise this laughter at the incongruity of her as the romantic Juliet would have hurt her more than it did. She took a deep breath and sat straighter. They'd laugh out of the other sides of their mouths when she read for the nurse. She'd show them!

"What part are you thinking of trying out for, Teresa?" Miss Eben asked.

"The nurse."

"Who else wants to try for the nurse?" The teacher looked at the girls. Not a hand was raised. "Very well, Teresa. You may do the nurse."

Tess felt as though she had been slapped in the face. She had been given the part because no one else wanted it, because she was so awkward and ungainly that even Miss Eben thought it was all she had the looks to do.

Donna squeezed her arm and whispered, "Wonderful, Tessie. You have a speaking part. I'm so glad."

Tess relaxed slightly, comforted by the warmth of her friend. But she *would* show them, she would indeed! She'd give them the best, the funniest, the homeliest nurse ever to say the lines! But, oh, how humiliating to get the part without even trying.

How could she tell Andy, after all the coaching he had given her? She scarcely heard the girls reading Juliet's lines.

Long after Uncle Will had gone to bed that night, she sat downstairs by the base-burner and learned her lines. If she was going to do a good job on this, she had to free herself from the book so she could really act. She found that many of her speeches had been cut from this high school version, but even so, she had a lot to learn and, when she got her back into it, this part was going to come alive. She wasn't a gravedigger for nothing! They'd find that Tess Trumper knew how to "dig" into Shakespeare too!

All agreed with Miss Eben that Ottilee Snyder was the right choice for Juliet. She was not only beautiful but also read the part feelingly. Donna remarked to Tess that she thought that all the trouble and suffering of the past year had given Ottilee more depth and understanding. To herself, Tess identified this as more of Miss Eben's character development showing itself in Ottilee.

Rehearsals went on every day after school. At first it all seemed a jumbled mess to Tess, everyone giggling and scuffling around on the stage, trying to carry out Miss Eben's directions. It was difficult for Tess to show off her learned lines in such confusion. She couldn't see how even Miss Eben was going to make anything out of it by the middle of April.

But by the middle of March the play began to take shape. Soon Tess found she was remembering more of the lines of other characters at every rehearsal. This, she supposed, was why Miss Eben liked them to do Shakespeare, it was such a good way to study him. Sometimes after she was in bed she would say Juliet's speeches and give Romeo's replies. What beauty in the lines! What love!

"My bounty is as boundless as the sea
My love as deep; the more I give to thee
The more I have, for both are infinite."

Compared to Juliet's, how flat seemed the lines of the nurse. But for every Juliet there had to be a nurse, she supposed, and for every Ottilee Snyder a Tess Trumper. Since she couldn't change her size or temperament, she'd better be philosophical. Nurses, horticulturists and, yes, certainly gravediggers, were very necessary. She wondered if she should tell Andy that she hadn't had to compete for her part at all. He seemed to have such a good opinion of her, she hated to spoil it.

The stage at Allerton high was small. In the crowd scenes, Miss Eben carefully outlined everyone's action so the actors without lines could all get on.

Costumes were handed out on April 3, with Miss Eben's instructions. They were to try them on at home and make the necessary adjustments. Tess eyed the bulky bundle of dark-brown material given her. Ugh! How ugly! And brown was her most unbecoming color. A piece of white material went with it, a wimple to be worn on her head, Miss Eben told her.

When she tried it on for Uncle Will's inspection, he gave her a long look. "Something's wrong with it, Tessie, but I don't know what. Why don't you take it over to Stella? She'll know where it ought to be taken in or let out."

Stella did. She pinned in a dart here, let out a seam there, and ripped out the hem to let it down.

"Good thing it's got a wide hem, Stella. I bet I'm the tallest nurse that ever wore this costume," Tess said as Stella sat on the floor to measure and pin the hem.

"And the best," Stella mumbled, her mouth full of pins.

When she finished, she got up and picked up the wimple. "Put this on your head, honey, and show me how you wear it. I'm going to wash it and starch it across the top so it'll stay in place."

First dress rehearsal came on April 10. Miss Eben wisely gave them time to take in one another's appearance, to get the laughter out of their systems. But no one laughed at Ottilee Snyder. Tess knew that Ottilee must be the most beautiful Juliet of all time. Her costumes were new, made for her by the Snyders' dressmaker. Long, flowing sleeves, diaphanous chiffon over satin, the little Juliet cap embroidered in pearls, Ottilee's mass of red, wavy hair hanging loose—well—even Miss Eben paused to take in the girl's beauty.

In the balcony scene, as Tess helped Ottilee up the ladder behind the set, she said, "Ottilee, I never imagined anyone could look so beautiful."

"Thanks, Tess, but it's just the costume. I think Mama overdid it, having them made especially. I only wish I were as good a Juliet as you are a nurse. Hope I don't fall off this ladder. All this flowing material is a real hazard."

"Don't worry, I'll be right here to steady it and catch you if you trip. Nursey is strong and will take care of her Juliet." Tess laughed softly.

"I know, Tess. You are so strong and reliable."

Tess stood on the ladder and listened to Romeo's famous lines as Ottilee stepped onto the shaky balcony.

"But soft, what light through yonder window breaks?
It is the East, and Juliet is the sun."

Strong and reliable! Adjectives of doom when one wanted to be beautiful, fascinating, and loved. Tess looked down at the voluminous folds of brown and ran her hand under her chin where the white cloth was fastened tightly. She wasn't going to have any trouble making the nurse seem sixty; in Ottilee's presence she felt more like a hundred.

It was seven o'clock before Tess got home on Wednesday, the twelfth. Everything had gone wrong at the last dress rehearsal. The balcony had tottered, she had climbed up to help Ottilee, Miss Eben had screamed for her to get back, that the balcony was only strong enough to hold Ottilee! Oh, it had been awful! She had even forgotten her lines and failed to call out on cue.

She found Andy in the kitchen with Uncle Will.

"Just wanted to tell you, I'm driving the carriage tomorrow night and I'll take you and Mr. Bagley to the play." Andy looked at her closely. "Anything wrong?"

"Just about everything! I don't think you should go. It's going to be a mess, just an awful mixed-up mess!" Tess wailed, dropping her coat on a chair.

"Good. I like a hearty laugh and high school Shakespeare sometimes provides the best. But, tomorrow, with an audience, I predict you'll all be fine, and the nurse a credit to us all. Don't forget that I, Andrew Herleman, Brutus, class of 1907, coached dear Nursey, so—she's got to be good."

Tess remembered his words on her first entrance the next night. She forgot the awful makeup Miss Eben had put on her face, all those wrinkle lines to make her look old. She just had to be good.

She entered, imitating Uncle Will's walk early in the morning before his joints loosened up. The little ripple of appreciative laughter was an invigorating breeze to her ego. She "put her back" into the part and, just as Andy had predicted, had the time of her life being the old, fuss-budget nurse. What fun it was to hear them laugh at her croaky voice and bustling manner. For the most part the play went well. The audience, a tolerant one, overlooked the trippings over robes and swords, the long pauses when lines were forgotten and the prompter had lost his place, the failure of the curtain to go all the way down at the end of a scene so that the scenery change was visible to all, and the sudden coming to life of Paris to arrange himself in a more comfortable position after he had been dead for sometime by Romeo's sword.

Tess stood in the wings to watch Juliet's awakening in the tomb. How lovely Ottilee looked lying there. All Juliets should have red hair, Tess thought. She did this scene so well; what agony in her lines as she discovered the body of Romeo.

> *"What's here? a cup, closed in my true love's hand?*
> *Poison, I see, hath been his timeless end.*
> *Oh churl! drunk all, and left no friendly drop*
> *To help me after? I will kiss thy lips;*
> *Haply some poison yet doth hang on them,*
> *To make me die with a restorative.*
> *Thy lips are warm."*

Tess felt a lump in her throat as Juliet took Romeo's dagger from his belt and stabbed herself. For the moment, Tess forgot that they were Ottilee Snyder and Johnny Hardy. Ottilee was certainly outdoing herself in tonight's performance.

The curtain down, Romeo and Paris on their feet, all was confusion backstage. Tess managed to get near Ottilee and squeeze her hand. "You are a real actress, Ottilee. Even made me cry just now, even though I've watched you do that scene so often and I know the lines as well as you do."

Ottilee's eyes were sparkling with success and excitement.

"Thanks Tess. But Juliet could not have managed without her nurse to lean on. You were wonderful."

Tess got out of her costume, rubbed her face with cold cream, and wiped off the wrinkles. The room was full of Shakespearean women changing back into high school girls.

Unnoticed, Tess left and walked down the hall toward the front door where she was to meet Uncle Will and Andy.

A voice called out, "Teresa, wait a minute." It was Miss Eben. Tess walked back. "Teresa, thank you. I have directed *Romeo and Juliet* seven times and this is the first time that the nurse has not given me trouble. I had thought of you for the part from the beginning, because you seem to have such a mature insight into character. No other girl could have brought the understanding to the part as you did. Thank you for a magnificent performance."

Tess was walking on air by the time she reached the front door. Parents, waiting for their actors, spoke to her, praising her acting skill.

When they got to Andy's carriage, he helped her into the front seat, although Uncle Will had sat there on the trip in from Willow Hill.

Uncle Will said how surprised he had been at seeing an old woman traipsing around on the stage instead of his Tessie, then he remained quiet in the back seat. Andy did enough talking for the three of them.

"I tell you, Tessie, seeing you up there made me as proud and excited as seeing one of my prize roses bloom for the first time. We'll have to watch this girl, Mr. Bagley, or she'll be leaving the cemetery and greenhouse to join a Shakespearean company." He reached over and squeezed her hand.

Tess had a crazy desire to whistle a tune and run up Willow Hill.

19. "Of a Sudden She Knows"

First-night errors corrected, the second performance went better. Miss Eben had two prompters holding books, one on each side. The only trouble was that, when a line was forgotten, the prompters vied with one another to supply the words, resulting in an audible duet that reached not only the actors but even the back row. Afterward, Linc told Tess that the prompters should have had parts, he could hear them better than some of the characters who mumbled.

But as a whole, Linc and Irene were delighted with the performance. Irene told Tess she was so proud of her she could just "bust." She and Linc, she said, had read the play together beforehand and so they doubly appreciated it.

Judge Milburn and Seth were there. And, to Tess's surprise, Stella, Sam, and Joe. Joe told her that Andy had given him tickets to take his parents.

Stella waited for her at the front door. "Honey," she said, "I didn't know you had it in you, up there spouting off all those words. Sam and I didn't get all that was going on, but it sure had a grand sound, especially when our Tessie stepped out."

Saturday morning when Tess opened her eyes, the world seemed dreary; the play was over; all that beautiful make-believe gone. How she wished they could do it again tonight. She sat on the edge of the bed and pulled on her stockings.

How thrilling it had been, receiving those compliments on her acting! Never had she had so much praise. She wished Andy had been there last night to see how much better she had done it. Thinking of Andy, she pulled on her shoes quickly and laced them. She'd try to get to the greenhouse early and tell him the details of last night's performance.

But at the greenhouse she found a strange Andy. He was quiet and had only short answers to her remarks. What had happened to him? Disappointed, she went into the greenhouse and started on the work he had ready for her. Joe also noticed Andy's detachment and asked Tess on the way home that night, "Do you suppose Mr. Andy's sick?"

"I don't know," she replied. Now her world *was* flat; no play and no Andy, at least not the friendly, jolly Andy whose sense of humor had given her such pleasure. What had happened to him? Maybe he had some trouble at home. She hoped he wasn't mad at her. Maybe he thought they had spent too many greenhouse hours on her play. Well, from now on she would work harder each Saturday to make up for it, then maybe he'd be as friendly as before.

At school they soon forgot the play and how, she, Teresa Trumper, had been such a fine character actress. She welcomed heavy spring work in the cemetery, donned her work clothes each afternoon with alacrity, and dug, mowed, and transplanted with even more than her usual robust energy. She did not sing, she did not whistle; she did not sit on the A B C stone to dream or to listen to the song of the willows.

Several times she noticed Uncle Will eying her speculatively as though he were about to question her moodiness. She was glad he held his tongue, for she herself did not know what had taken hold of her, why living all of a sudden was so tasteless. She bought a new tailored suit with the money she had saved, but wearing it to church on Sunday, and being told by Uncle Will that she looked stunning, failed to lift her spirits.

Each Saturday morning she went to the greenhouse, hoping to find the old Andy, but he wasn't there; there was just a man, her employer—efficient, businesslike, and reserved. Once she looked up suddenly from a funeral wreath she was making and, seated at his desk, he was looking at her with such a pained expression that she hurt in her throat at the misery of it. What was it? Oh, if only Mama were here or Irene, so she could talk over this strange agony she felt inside.

Judge Milburn came out May 7 and was pleased with the appearance of his lot. "It'll be beautiful by Decoration Day, Tess," he said. "School going well?" Tess nodded. "When is graduation?"

"Friday, May 26."

"I'll be there with bells on to see you get that diploma."

When he left, Tess walked up to the top of the hill wondering why the thought of the long-coveted diploma brought little satisfaction.

The seniors were given the last week off. Tess was grateful for the extra time to help Uncle Will get ready for Decoration Day. Spring had come again and the cemetery was green and blooming, but Tess saw only the dirt she cultivated and the dead branches she pruned.

On Wednesday after lunch, Uncle Will said, "Tessie, I just put up the hammock. You did enough work this morning. Now I want you to spend the afternoon lying in the hammock. You've been looking kind of puny lately. I'd like for you to perk up for your graduation. My, how Agnes looked forward to the day you'd graduate from high school."

"Oh, Uncle Will, I'm not tired, not at all. I planned to work in the potter's field this afternoon and I want to do some things on the Washingtons' lot, especially on little Rachel's grave."

"Her folks will want to do that. You are to lie in the hammock and read a book. You hear?"

"Yes, Uncle Will."

She put on a clean dress, went to the bookcase to get the book Uncle Will had ordered. Uninterestedly she took the first one at hand, the book lying on top of the others. It was *The Little Minister*. She remembered now that she had put it there hurriedly after Andy had returned it, intending to tuck it later into its proper place on a lower shelf.

She lay in the hammock and idly flipped the pages. The sight of underscored passages and the memory of Andy's remark brought her to a sitting position.

"Your mother must have been a wonderful, sensitive woman," he had said, referring to these same underscorings.

Tess went through chapter by chapter and read the parts Mama had liked so much. But it was one in Chapter Twenty-three that stopped her!

The author was writing of the wild, beautiful, mischievous, unpredictable little Babbie, who, in spite of all her faults and misdemeanors, the little minister could not help loving.

"No woman is so bad but we may rejoice when her heart thrills to love, for then God has her by the hand. There is no love but this. She may dream of what love is, but it is only of a sudden that she knows."

Tess put her hand to her throat. Of a sudden she knew. She was in love! Big, tall, ungainly Tess Trumper was in love with a man who could never love her because she was a giant! Oh, why couldn't she have been the size of little Babbie or Irene or Ottilee? Why was she such a freak?

She jumped up, dropped the book in the hammock, and ran up the hill, tears stinging her eyes all the way.

Under the willows she sat on the stone, put her head on her knees, and cried as she had not done since Mama's death. Her deep sobs kept her from hearing the swish of the willows and approaching footsteps.

"Tessie, Tessie, what is it? What's wrong?" Irene dropped down beside her. "I was visiting Mama and then came over here to tell you the news and find you like this. Is Uncle Will sick? Did you fail your examinations? What is it? Oh, please stop crying!" Irene put her arm about Tess.

"Oh, Irene, it's so awful! I hurt so and I don't know what to do about it!"

"If you're sick, let's go see Mama, she'll know what to do."

"Stella can't help this sickness. Irene, I'm in love!"

Irene dropped her arm from Tess's shoulder. "Well, good! It's about time. I was beginning to think you weren't human on that score. But why all the tears? You should be walking on a pink cloud."

"Oh, Irene, it's all so hopeless. He could never love me. He just thinks of me as the big girl who helps out in his greenhouse."

"You mean Andy Herleman?"

Tess nodded miserably.

"How do you know you are in love with him?"

Tess took the handkerchief Irene handed her and wiped her eyes. "Well, all along I've liked being with him. He's so good-natured and he makes me feel important; he has seemed to enjoy talking to me. And then, all of sudden, right after the play, he was different. Now he scarcely talks to me at all and then only when Joe is around. I have been feeling just awful, but until Mama spoke to me just now in something she had underscored in *The Little Minister,* I didn't know I was in love. Oh, Irene, it's so hopeless, I'm such a tall string bean."

Irene took her hand. "Does it bother you, Tess, that Andy is short?"

"Of course not. I'd love him no matter what his size, he's such a fine man."

"Did it ever occur to you that he might be in love with you but thinks you could not care for him because of *his* size?"

Tess thought this over. "You mean this recent reserve is to cover up his real feeling for me?" Irene nodded. "But, Irene, how can I let him know how I feel without being bold about it? Stella always told us 'Never forget to be a lady.'"

"Sure, but you can let him know in subtle ways that you are fond of him."

Tess sighed. "If it were only *just* fond, I could stand it. But, Irene! What if he doesn't care? And, I *must* face it, how could he?"

"Tessie, Tessie, where is all your self-confidence? Where's Agnes Trumper's daughter who has been able to tackle anything? Now, let's get down to brass tacks. Think of something Andy likes especially, something you could do or say that would show him you are catering to his preferences."

Tess reached up and pushed in a loosened hairpin. "Well, I was going to wear my white Sunday dress for commencement on Friday. Once he said he wished I'd wear my yellow one. He saw me in it that time last July. You remember, I told you."

"Well, then, wear it."

"But how will he know that I'm doing it for him? The way he's been acting toward me, I'm sure he won't even go to the graduation."

"Trust a little in fate, Tessie. I did, and it brought Linc. Now,

Miss Weepy, do you think you could spare a moment to hear *my* news?"

"Oh, Irene, I'm a clod! What a blubbering, love-sick idiot I am, not to ask you. Tell me, what's happened?"

"Well, my first news is, we are leaving Mrs. Converse the first of June. Maybe you don't know it, but Mrs. Snyder owns the Glasser Building just off the downtown square on East Third. The first of May, one of the store rooms in it became vacant. She came to Linc and offered to rent it to him for our business. She has helped us get a loan at the bank for the equipment we'll need, glass cases, scales, a good range for one of the back rooms where we'll prepare the food, and a few other things we'll need.

"For the time being," Irene went on, "we'll live in the other back room. With no house rent to pay, we'll get ahead faster, get the loan paid off. Both Mrs. Snyder and Mrs. Converse are sure we'll make a go of it. They have promised to buy food for their parties from us. And I'm sure others will follow their lead. There's never been a place like it in Allerton. People will always go where there is good food for sale and we aim for our food to be the best."

"Golly, Irene, I'm so happy for you. I can just see you and Linc, all dressed in spotless white, waiting on a crowd of customers. Your shop will be filled with good smells, baked ham, potato salad made from Aunt Belinda's recipe, and your wonderful nut bread. You must leave the door open as often as possible. The good odors will bring in customers."

Irene laughed. "Now you sound like Tess."

Tess frowned. "I guess it's easy to be optimistic about other people's future. But say, you said that was your first news. What's the second?"

Irene smiled radiantly. "How would you like to be Aunt Tessie to our first-born, early in 1912?"

"Irene!" Tess exploded, her misery forgotten. "A baby! Gee whilickers! How could you keep quiet about that all this time? Me and my big complaining mouth! When do you think it will be? What are you going to name it? What did Stella say?"

Irene answered Tess's questions proudly.

It was late afternoon before they parted, each filled with an inner warmth at having shared one another's intimate joys and problems.

Comforted by Irene's advice, Tess picked up the book from the hammock, returned it to the bookcase and went to the kitchen to prepare supper.

After the meal she built up the fire in the kitchen stove. Uncle Will asked the reason.

"I'm going to heat the irons and press my yellow dress. I've decided to wear it for commencement." She got out the ironing board.

Uncle Will folded back a page of his newspaper. "Thought you were going to wear the white one."

"No, Andy likes the yellow."

Uncle Will looked at her over the top of his spectacles, but said nothing.

Friday was a fine day. Since her talk with Irene, Tess felt so much better that, early in the afternoon, she even hummed a little along with the tune of the lawn mower as she worked on the south slope.

She returned to the house about three to take a bath and dress for the big event in the evening. Uncle Will was in the kitchen.

"I built up the fire and put the water on for your bath," he told her.

"Oh, thanks, Uncle Will."

"You're welcome. And thank *you* for laying out my good suit. I stepped over to the greenhouse awhile ago," he went on casually. "Had to tell Andy about the evergreen he set out on the Tompkins' lot. It's not doing well, you know."

Tess nodded and watched his face. She knew that look. What had he been up to?

"Asked Andy if he was going to attend the exercises tonight and he said he guessed not." Tess felt a rock drop kerplunk in her stomach. She turned away as Uncle Will went on. "I told him that was too bad because you were wearing your yellow dress because he liked it. Well, sir, he brightened up like all get-out and said he probably would go after all and would we like for him to come after us in his carriage. I said yes, but if you'd rather we went on the streetcar, I'll phone him."

Tess threw her arms around her uncle. "Uncle Will, did I ever tell you what a lamb you are? Skedaddle out of here this minute so I can take a bath."

Andy drove up about six-forty-five. Tess met him on the porch. He handed her a box.

"I made up a bouquet for you, Tess, as soon as your uncle told me what dress you were wearing."

Tess opened the box and caught her breath at the lavender sweet peas and yellow roses. "Andy, Andy, how beautifully you arranged them and how sweet they smell!" She took out the flowers.

Andy reached up to his coat lapel and took out a long pin and handed it to her. "Will this be about right to fasten them to your belt?"

By the time she had fastened on the flowers, Uncle Will had already crawled into the back seat. Andy helped her over the front wheel. The drive into town had never seemed so short, nor the streets so beautiful. What magic in a yellow dress. Bless that Irene!

Seated alphabetically on the stage, Ottilee Snyder was next to Tess. Ottilee's dress was pale green, her flowers, pink roses. She whispered to Tess that it was fortunate that the colors of their dresses looked well together.

The house lights were on and Tess could see four Washingtons seated on the side near the front—Stella, Sam, Seth and Joe—and beside them, Irene and Linc. Just back of them sat Judge Milburn, Uncle Will, and Andy.

All of these people here because of her! It was like having a big family. How happy Stella must be about Irene's baby. It would help ease the loss of Rachel.

And Andy, how did he feel about her? He had seemed more like himself tonight. She certainly had tried to let him know how she felt about him, by glance and voice. She hoped she hadn't been a coquette. That would have been all wrong, unsuitable for a person like herself and an unsuitable way to express the depth of feeling she had for him. He mustn't think her a flirt. Oh, she hoped he didn't misunderstand her!

She scarcely heard Johnny Hardy's long-winded, memorized speech, nor the music, nor the recitation by Virgil Leach called, "The Road Ahead."

She heard the principal call out "Teresa Bagley Trumper." Remembering Stella's words, "proud to be tall," she held her head high as she walked across the stage to receive her diploma, the faint sweetness of the flowers at her waist wafting up to her nose.

The spring night had grown cool by the time they started home. Andy put her coat around her shoulders. She held her diploma in her lap.

"Well, Tessie," Uncle Will said from the rear seat, "only one thing could have made me happier and that would have been to have Agnes see you. I declare, when I saw you walking across that stage so straight and pretty, my eyes just puddled up, yes sir, just puddled up. Agnes said to me just the week before she died, 'See that she gets an education, Will.' And now we've done it, Tess, just like she wanted."

"Let's just say we got the diploma, Uncle Will. It will depend on what I do with what I learned that will show whether I got an education or not. Now Andy, here, is the one with education; he runs a greenhouse, coaches a Shakespearean actress, helps an eighth-grade boy with his homework, and land knows what else."

Andy laughed. "Tessie, flattery will get you nowhere. You are *not* going to rehearse Lady Macbeth in the morning. You and I are going to spread fertilizer in those outside beds. Now, how's that for coming out of the clouds and down to earth with a bang?"

"I'll love spreading fertilizer, Mr. Herleman," Tess returned, wanting to add—with you. Instead she laughed and leaned down to sniff the sweet peas.

After Andy had left them on the porch, Uncle Will unlocked the door and went in to light a lamp.

"Uncle Will," Tess called in through the screen, "I'm going to take a run up the hill before going to bed. I'm too excited to sleep yet."

She slipped her arms into the sleeves of her coat and dropped her diploma in Uncle Will's porch chair. In the starlight the road up the hill was before her like a beckoning light. She did not run, but sauntered up, noting her silent friends on either side; the Hanrahans, the Wallaces, the Georges, the Kimbles, the Milburns, the Manlys, the Andersons, the Snyders, the Jewetts, and all the others beyond the roadside.

The world was as much a part of them as of the living, she thought, just as she was a part of Agnes and Jimpson Trumper. The world was a long chain; she was only one link, a strong one she hoped, one that wouldn't break under pressure.

At the top of the hill she sat on the A B C stone. Removing her flowers, she fastened her coat against the chill of the wind. She held the bouquet to her cheek.

"I did it, Mama, got the diploma," she said softly. "And they all saw me, Uncle Will and the rest—and—and Andy. I think he *does* like me, Mama. I really do. Hope you approve of him."

The willow branches swayed in the wind, the leaves rustled, and Tess heard the whispered reply.

About the Author

Elisabeth Hamilton Friermood has the happy faculty of writing books that both her readers and the reviewers greet with enthusiasm. Most of her books have period settings, and many have the Midwest as a background. WHISPERING WILLOWS deals with the scene of her own girlhood, early-twentieth-century Indiana. Her first of many popular novels for young people was published by Doubleday in 1951.

Mrs. Friermood, who is a native of Marion, Indiana, studied at Northwestern University and the University of Wisconsin. She was children's librarian in Marion and in Dayton, Ohio, before moving to New York in 1944. Her husband, Dr. Harold T. Friermood, is the National Director for Health and Physical Education of the Y.M.C.A. The Friermoods and their daughter live in Pelham, New York.